SAVE YOUR TEARS

Donna McGuire is trying to run the ranch she inherited from her Texan grandfather. But she is black-listed in the community, unable to obtain any credit. Someone is sabotaging her business. Could it be her grandfather's trusted friend, the handsome Jared Jackson, who has made no secret of the fact that he finds her incompetent and wants her land? And what is she to do about Amy-Kate, Jared's small daughter, who is determinedly looking for a new Mamma . . . ?

Books by Beverley Winter in the Linford Romance Library:

HOUSE ON THE HILL
A TIME TO LOVE
LOVE UNDERCOVER
MORTIMER HOUSE
THE HEART'S LONGING
LOVE ON SAFARI
WOMAN WITH A MISSION
BUTTERFLY LADY
SEASON OF SECRETS
A BRIDE FOR JASON

BEVERLEY WINTER

SAVE YOUR TEARS

Complete and Unabridged

LINFORD
Leicester

First published in Great Britain in 2007

First Linford Edition
published 2008

British Library CIP Data

Winter, Beverley
Save your tears.—Large print ed.—
Linford romance library
1. Ranch life—Texas—Fiction
2. Inheritance and succession—Fiction
3. Love stories 4. Large type books
I. Title
823.9′2 [F]

ISBN 978–1–84782–075–4

Published by
F. A. Thorpe (Publishing)
Anstey, Leicestershire

Set by Words & Graphics Ltd.
Anstey, Leicestershire
Printed and bound in Great Britain by
T. J. International Ltd., Padstow, Cornwall

This book is printed on acid-free paper

1

The sky was like brass, burnished to a deep gold by the fierce afternoon sun. The girl in the blue Chevrolet pickup viewed the flat, dusty landscape stretching for vast distances on either side of the road and tried not to think about the merciless heat invading the cab.

Even the air conditioning appeared to be making no difference as the sun poured in through the glass, baking the fair skin on her arms and shoulders to a deep rose. What's more, it had audaciously summoned one or two freckles to her face, and there was nothing she hated more than freckles!

She ran slender fingers through her abundant dark hair in a futile attempt to cool herself, lifting its shoulder-length weight from her gently perspiring neck.

The pink sundress she'd purchased hurriedly that morning was skimpy enough, with thin shoulder straps and a mini skirt, but even this was not cool enough.

Why hadn't the travel agent warned her that Texas in August would be a total inferno?

Despite her discomfort, she couldn't prevent the happy glint in her sapphire eyes, or the wily smile which enhanced her already flawless features into what her grandfather would call 'unrivalled Celtic beauty, to be sure . . . '

'So far, so good,' she gloated softly. 'Not bad at all for a girl who dislikes polluted cities and crowded airports. Donna-Marie McGuire, for a country mouse from a small Irish village you're quite something, dashing to the other side of the world like this at a moment's notice.'

Her overnight flight with American Airlines to Dallas Fort Worth International Airport had been hassle-free and she could now savour the heady feelings of excitement and anticipation which bubbled inside her.

SPECIAL MESSAGE TO READERS

This book is published under the auspices of

THE ULVERSCROFT FOUNDATION

(registered charity No. 264873 UK)

Established in 1972 to provide funds for research, diagnosis and treatment of eye diseases.

Examples of contributions made are: —

A Children's Assessment Unit at Moorfield's Hospital, London.

•

Twin operating theatres at the Western Ophthalmic Hospital, London.

•

A Chair of Ophthalmology at the Royal Australian College of Ophthalmologists.

•

The Ulverscroft Children's Eye Unit at the Great Ormond Street Hospital For Sick Children, London.

You can help further the work of the Foundation by making a donation or leaving a legacy. Every contribution, no matter how small, is received with gratitude. Please write for details to:

THE ULVERSCROFT FOUNDATION,
The Green, Bradgate Road, Anstey,
Leicester LE7 7FU, England.
Telephone: (0116) 236 4325

In Australia write to:

THE ULVERSCROFT FOUNDATION,
c/o The Royal Australian and New Zealand College of Ophthalmologists,
94-98 Chalmers Street, Surry Hills,
N.S.W. 2010, Australia

'Forty-eight hours,' she mused. That's all it had taken to make her decision, store her furniture and hand back the cottage keys to her landlord, Connor McGrewar, with the announcement that she was leaving the lush, emerald isle of her birth. It had been no mean feat.

Connor McGrewar, bless his hand-made leather brogues, had been downright peeved. Not only would he have to find a new tenant for the cottage, but the stunning Ms McGuire was running out on him after only two days.

'Why Texas, for Pete's sake?' he'd exploded. To annoy her further he'd added nastily, 'I daresay Irish men aren't good enough for the likes of you. You'll be wantin' the excitement of a bunch of sweaty cowboys. Well, darlin', I wish you joy of them!'

Unwilling to give him the satisfaction of knowing how much these unfair comments had hurt her, she'd smiled sweetly. 'Goodbye, Connor. I do hope that one day you will get a life.'

He'd given her a long, hard stare.

'Don't think you've seen the last of me, Donna sweetheart, because I always get what I want.' And what he wanted right now more than Donna herself was to be able to take her down a peg or three, the snooty little cat! Even if it meant following her to Texas.

'I'll need a forwarding address,' he'd said cunningly, 'so I can send on any mail.'

Donna wasn't born yesterday. 'You may redirect any letters to my sister in England,' she'd told him crisply.

If Connor intended to make a nuisance of himself, at least she could count on Seonaid to give him short shrift.

The Texas sun continued to pour into the cab of the pickup as mile after melting mile the dusty plains rolled by. Donna became even more wretchedly uncomfortable.

However, even the unaccustomed heat could not dim that earlier glow of satisfaction. Since her arrival she'd managed to hire a reliable vehicle (if one didn't count the air conditioning, that is), negotiate her way to a supermarket on the outskirts of Forth Worth where she'd purchased a paper sack full of groceries (her grandfather was bound to need supplies because an ailing old man living on his own needed all the help he could get), and then head south on the interstate towards San Antonio.

Opposite the supermarket she'd found a fascinating little shop which sold Western gear, and twenty minutes later she'd returned to the car, the proud owner of three pairs of jeans, four pretty, western-style blouses, a pair of soft leather boots and a cream felt cowboy hat.

Unfortunately these purchases, including the pink sundress, had made rather a dent in her savings. But the fact was she needed to look the part. It might even be a good idea to stop somewhere and change out of her sundress and sandals. One didn't arrive at a cattle ranch dressed for a day on the beach.

She sighed. Not that Grandfather

would notice what she wore. The poor old dear would be ensconced in his sick bed, wearily fading away.

As the pickup ate up the miles Donna considered that she'd chosen well when it came to the dark blue Chevrolet. As far as she was concerned a vehicle could be any make under the sun as long as the colour was right. The man at the hire firm had been amazed when she'd refused the red saloon, but orange-red just wasn't her colour.

Dark blue, on the other hand, matched her eyes. She'd explained to the clerk that she was very particular about these things. She liked her surroundings to be colour co-ordinated.

'Eyes of blue and a lass that's true . . . ' she crooned rather sentimentally in a rich contralto voice.

It was a song her grandfather had made up for her when she was a small girl, sitting on his knee, and brought back happy memories of holidays at the ranch on the few occasions when her parents had been able to afford them.

Without being conceited Donna knew that her eyes were her best feature; large, heavily lashed and 'sapphire-going-on-navy', as Grandfather would say.

As her thoughts turned to the small west coast town she'd left behind, Donna experienced an unexpected pang of homesickness. Already she was missing the emerald fields of sheep and horses, the rocky sea cliffs where the gulls keened and the constant drizzle against her windows. She was even missing her goat, Ermintrude.

Ermintrude had resided in the rented paddock next to the cottage, happily sharing the henhouse with three hens and two ducks. On Donna's departure her neighbour, Mrs Fitzpatrick, had been happy to take over the animals.

They would be well cared for, but this fact in no way prevented her from remembering them with sharp longing. She could just see the fat white bodies of Daisy and Loverduck as they waddled about in the mud . . .

Donna couldn't help but contrast the scene in her mind with the dry, unfamiliar landscape before her. It was all so strange; everything from the fierce, burning heat to the vast open spaces; the prickly cactus plants and the fields of wild sunflowers as gold as the sunshine pouring over them.

Then there was the deep, slow drawl of the men and the lazy nasal twang of the women she'd met in the shops that morning. And as for driving on the 'wrong' side of the road . . . well, the less said about that the better. She'd made it this far without mishap and she wasn't about to tempt fate!

'No use pining for home, Donna,' she told herself firmly, 'this is your home, now.' She'd made her decision and there would be no turning back. Besides, as an orphan, she had no other family left in Eire.

Her elder sister, Seonaid, was married to a London stockbroker and although the sisters adored one another they had very little in common. Seonaid was a city girl. She was also a high-powered barrister with rather a lot to say for herself. The path she had chosen was not for Donna.

Seonaid loved the high life and lived amongst the mink-and-manure set in Surrey, whereas Donna preferred to opt for the real thing. Real manure, that is, with the warm, sweet smell of hay and the soft breath of horses waiting to be fed in the barn.

Which was precisely why she was here at this moment, driving west to her grandfather's cattle ranch near the Frio River in her smart, colour co-ordinated pickup.

Did she say Grandfather's ranch? By all accounts it was soon to be hers and Seonaid's. Her grandfather had written to inform her of his failing health, suggesting that she pay him a visit as soon as she could. It was years since he'd seen his family, he'd said, sounding forlorn, and Donna's kind heart had been touched. Besides that, if, as his only surviving relatives, she and Seonaid were to inherit the Double Circle Ranch upon his death, one of them had better start learning about ranching.

Seonaid had been horrified. 'Darling, I have no intention of getting involved with a bunch of sweaty, uncouth cowboys and their vicious, longhorn steers. And as for Texas, it's full of deadly rattlesnakes and those filthy mesquite bushes, or had you forgotten? Their thorns tore us to shreds when we were little! If you wish to live in that funny little log house of Grandfather's and be torn to shreds you may do so, but count me out.'

'Even for a visit?'

'Even for a visit.' Her voice had come firmly down the telephone line, crisp with annoyance.

'But Seonaid, when Grandfather dies we'll be co-owners. I want to keep my half and I couldn't possibly afford to buy you out. I'm not wealthy like you.'

Her sister had made an impatient sound. It was getting late and she was dining at the manor with Lord and Lady Huntley-Hatton that evening.

'I'm giving you my half share, Donna. I don't want it. Just don't come whining to me in a year's time saying you've made a mistake, that's all. Are you quite sure you want to go in for this ranching lark?'

'Quite sure.'

'May I remind you that it's a hard life. You'll be completely at sea, my dear. You know nothing about ranching.'

'I'm a fast learner. I intend to turn Grandfather's 'spread' into an even bigger success. I know it'll probably be a bit run-down to start with, what with his being ill and not able to cope very well, but I'll soon fix that. I'll work hard and Grandpa will be proud of me. It's the least I can do for him, and for Dad and Mum's memory. Mum may have been an Irish colleen, but Dad was Texan to his toenails.'

'Ah, but his ancestors were Irish,' Seonaid had reminded her smugly.

'Even so. Once a rancher, always a rancher. He only agreed to live in Ireland with Mum because she was so unhappy in the heat, and missed the green countryside.'

'Look, Donna, I must go. Do what you like . . . be a cowgirl if that's what you want, but don't blame me if it doesn't work out.'

'Don't worry about me Seonaid. I've thought a lot about it since Grandfather's letter, and it really is what I want to do with my life. Perhaps it's the Texan half of me, but I couldn't stay away from the Double Circle Ranch now if I tried . . . '

⋆ ⋆ ⋆

Wearily Donna looked at her watch. It was later than she'd thought; almost five. The sky was still a bright bowl overhead and it looked set to stay that way for another two hours at least. She wrinkled her perfect little nose and glanced in the rear-view mirror in an effort to determine how many freckles had appeared in the last half hour.

During the long flight she'd taken the trouble to memorise the route and realised that she still had quite a way to go. Lunch, a hamburger and French fries from a fast-food outlet near Austin, seemed a long time ago. Her insides were beginning to rumble but with any luck she'd be at the Double Circle by dinner time.

She put her foot down hard on the accelerator. 'There's no time to waste, Donna McGuire . . . '

But instead of increasing speed the Chevrolet gave an ominous splutter and refused to comply. In vain Donna pumped the accelerator.

'Now what . . . ?' she muttered in frustration.

One glance at the dashboard revealed the source of her problem, and her eyes widened in disbelief. How could she have been so careless? The tank had been full when she'd left the airport, and now it was empty. In her excitement she'd neglected to keep an eye on mundane things like petrol gauges.

With an obstinate cough the pickup eased itself to the side of the road and rolled to a halt. Resignedly Donna switched off the ignition. 'Everything had been going so well,' she sighed, drumming her immaculate pink-tipped fingers on the steering wheel, 'and now this! Take a deep breath and don't panic, Donna-Marie McGuire. It's not the end of the world, even a big one like Texas. Just try to think . . . '

Helplessly she stared out of the window. There wasn't a living soul in sight. The landscape was filled with cedars and live oak trees, with the paler green of the thorny mesquite bushes interspersed between them.

Even the brush alongside the road was thick, filled with prickly cactus plants and fierce-looking yucca. Not a place to attempt to wade through, she thought morosely, even if there was a ranch house within reach somewhere.

A few miles back she remembered passing vast, cultivated fields of red-tipped maize and some knee high corn, but even then there hadn't been a dwelling in sight. Right here there wasn't even a maize field. There was simply . . . nothing! Unless you counted the odd windmill or oil derrick which dotted the flat countryside.

Furious with herself for her oversight, Donna tried once again to marshal her thoughts. She had no mobile telephone with her so she couldn't even contact the Double Circle Ranch for advice. Worse . . . it wasn't as though Grandfather would muster a search party for her when she didn't arrive because he didn't actually know she was coming! It had been foolish, perhaps, not to inform him, but she'd wanted her arrival to come as a lovely surprise.

There was nothing for it but to sit and wait for another car to come along. And that, she realised in some dismay, might well take hours. Of course, she could always start walking to the nearest signs of habitation but in this heat she wouldn't get very far. Ranches in this part of the world were spread out over thousands of acres; they were literally worlds apart.

Donna swallowed. 'Uh-oh, I feel a headache coming on . . . '

Making a valiant effort to control the rising panic, she rubbed her temples with her fingertips. She was determined not to cry despite the small sob of fatigue and frustrations rising in her throat. Leaning forward, she rested her head on her arms, at the same time squeezing her eyes shut tightly.

It wasn't long before jetlag combined with the stress of the past forty-eight hours and an uncomfortable night sitting upright in the aircraft between two elderly people who snored began to take its toll.

Exhaustion claimed her. Within a few seconds Donna McGuire, self-confessed traveller of the most intrepid kind, was soundly asleep.

A banging noise on the window alongside one ear penetrated her unconscious state. Donna murmured drowsily and tried to go back to sleep, but the noise continued. She lifted her head, blinked owlishly and gasped.

On the other side of the glass window was the coldest pair of grey eyes she had ever seen, viewing her from a handsome, outraged face.

The face belonged to a tall man who straightened to his full height and continued to observe her narrowly, both hands thrust aggressively into the pockets of his work-stained jeans. He was large, dark and intimidating, and scrutiny left Donna in no doubt that he regarded her as an inferior life form . . . probably something disgusting and squirmy under a stone.

Donna took an instant dislike to him. Who did the man think he was, waking her up from a deep sleep when she was so tired? Cautiously she wound down the window for all of two inches, conscious of a tight knot of apprehension forming in her stomach. She was all alone in a foreign country, and totally vulnerable.

'Yes? What do you want?'

Despite the sleepy note her low, husky voice cracked a little with fear. Did those light grey eyes really entice the soul out of her, almost ready to absorb her every thought?

As she stared at him he lifted his black cowboy hat a fraction and ran a hand through his thick, dark hair. Carefully he settled the hat more firmly on his head, an action which gave him time to get his breath back. Who was this crazy woman who'd been baking herself in a cab of a pickup on a day like this? She both looked and sounded like every dream he'd ever had all rolled into one and he didn't like it one bit. No sir.

'Howdy, Ma'am,' he drawled, 'something wrong?'

Despite the polite words spoken in a

deep, Texan voice, his irritation was obvious.

Defiantly Donna straightened her back. She glared right back, fright and fatigue winning out over good manners. Besides that, her head was beginning to throb abominably.

'Don't you have anything better to do than accost innocent women as they take a nap?' she snapped. 'Do go away, whoever you are . . . I have no time for Peeping Toms!'

The grey eyes became arctic. 'You married, Ma'am?'

Donna blinked. How rude could the man get? 'What's it to you?' she hissed. 'The answer is no, and I'm not likely to be either, if you are an example of the type of arrogant, disapproving male one could expect to meet in these parts.'

He smiled nastily. 'Then some poor jerk has had a fortunate escape. As a wife you'd be an utter nag.'

Donna gasped. 'Well, really! What a thing to say . . . '

They glared at one another like two

dogs spoiling for a fight, but when Donna's gaze lowered to his sternly set mouth she was amazed to see it twitch. The wretch appeared to be finding some amusement in the situation.

'It ain't usual practice for a female to take a nap at this time of day on the roadside,' he pointed out reasonably.

'No? Well, I'm not your average female.'

'It would be failing in common decency if I did not warn you that it's unsafe for a woman to be on her own in the middle of nowhere,' he growled. 'This is harsh country.'

Unable to prevent a yawn, she attempted to hide it behind her pretty, pink-tipped fingers, then closed her eyes and rubbed her forehead in a futile attempt to ease the ache.

The man continued to regard her expressionlessly. It was amazing how pretty women often had the attention span of a fruitfly. Heck, what did he do now? He couldn't very well leave her alone.

Donna looked up at his inscrutable face and felt the unaccountable need to make some sort of explanation. Perhaps then he'd go away and leave her in peace.

'I was tired so I decided to have a sleep. That's hardly a crime, is it?'

In the silence which followed she was feminine enough to take another quick peek at his face from beneath her thick, dark lashes. Despite herself she was impressed. His light grey eyes were startling against the deep tan of his face; an arresting face, craggily handsome, with lean cheeks and a tough, determined jaw.

He seemed to have an aura of masculine self-sufficiency which was attractive and yet somehow menacing; obviously a man who knew what he wanted, had the ability to get it and then simply took it. No problem.

There was an incredible amount of machismo packed into that powerful body, and something almost arrogant in the set of his head and shoulders. The shoulders were as wide as all Texas, too.

'You were tired?' He looked knowing and disdainful at the same time.

'Yeah,' Donna insisted, sounding like a third grader who hadn't done her homework and was trying to bluff it out. 'Very tired.'

Unable to prevent herself, she yawned once more behind her hand. 'Oh, do excuse me, the truth is I had very little sleep last night. I was with this elderly man who snored like a chainsaw and I hadn't the heart to wake him, besides the fact that I didn't know him well enough . . .'

The man's jaw tightened. 'You were with an old man?' he asked incredulously, adding cynically, 'I take it y'all had a good time, then.'

Donna didn't care for the jeering note in his voice. She watched as he clamped his mouth shut in an obvious effort to prevent himself from saying anything further. Something, she had no doubt, which would have been extremely uncomplimentary.

To be honest, it wasn't that she was averse to flying; it was just that she objected to the cramped seating in economy class, and not being able to have a decent night's sleep.

His firm lips compressed into a tight line of disapproval. 'You don't say.' Donna couldn't think why he was looking so put out. It wasn't often she had this affect on a man!

'Are you one of those misguided females who find their entertainment by offering comfort to elderly oil barons with more money than sense. Or, heaven help them, to the fame-hungry cowboys willing to break their bones on the circuit each week for a fancy medal and a few miserable dollars which they then go and blow in the nearest saloon.'

The man must be mad, Donna thought. She'd been conversing with a madman, and she was all alone with him in the middle of West Texas! She had no idea what he was talking about and yet she could have sworn that there was a quite rational man beneath all that crazy talk.

Donna took a deep breath. Thank goodness she'd had the foresight to lock her door. All she needed to do now was close the window.

'If you ask me,' he continued darkly, 'a man has a lot more neck to risk on an Alley Bat than on ridin' a bull or wrestlin' a steer. Some men,' he finished in a low, bitter voice, 'never learn.'

'Er, no,' Donna agreed weakly. The knot in her stomach tightened further as she glanced at the green sports utility vehicle parked directly in front of her blue Chevrolet. If only she could get him to take his fancy Lincoln away and leave her in peace to think about the predicament she was in, she would be OK . . . but she couldn't think straight while he was scaring her half to death with all that gobbledegook.

She wound the window up another two inches and pointed. 'That yours? Hadn't you better be on your way?'

Then because she was so desperately thirsty, begged without thinking, 'got any water? I'm dying of thirst.'

He rolled his eyes to heaven. By her accent the woman was not from Texas. What did a dumb foreigner know?

'Sure you are,' he agreed. 'You're probably dehydrated. You'd do well to do what we Texans do. We always carry our own drinks with us when we travel.'

He enlightened her further. 'Drought is a fact of life in these parts, lady. We only get a couple of inches of rain a year so our windmills have to go full tilt to haul up the water from way underground.'

Much as he detested money grabbers, he felt compelled to help her. Besides, to a hungry man she had a voice like warm honey pouring over a breakfast pancake. It was a pity she was such an obvious airhead. Only a dim city-bred female would boil herself to death inside a cab while she caught up on her beauty sleep and then expect not to get thirsty enough to drink sheep dip!

Unable to stop himself, his eyes roved over Donna's arms and shoulders. That deliciously pink skin was already showing signs of some ugly sunburn. Come the morning and she'd be one cooked coyote, all right.

With a sigh he turned and strode towards his vehicle, yanked open the door and removed a can of pop from the cool box on the back seat. As he did so Donna had a good view of his lithe, powerful body and the jeans which were very pleasing to the eye, fitting his strongly muscled legs like an indigo glove.

On his return she wound the window down another few inches, grabbed the can he'd opened for her, and drank thirstily.

'That was wonderful. Thank you very much,' she gasped, wiping her mouth rather inelegantly on the back of her hand. The smile she bestowed on him was so bewitching that he took a hasty step backwards.

Her accent on top of the smile was knocking him sideways . . . was it an Irish lilt? Irish or not, he told himself firmly, she needn't think he was susceptible to any foreign, feminine charm. This here was one big Texan who was mighty wised-up.

Donna eyed him sadly. It had been no pleasure at all, even she could see that. He was lying through his teeth, and she had no time for men who lied.

'Now that you're . . . properly awake, you'd better be on your way,' he advised her tersely.

Her eyes, he mused, were the most incredible blue, like the national flower of Texas which came up each summer in his fields, those gorgeous Bluebonnets with their proud, straight stalks.

Remembering her plight, desperation made Donna bolt. 'I wonder if I could trouble you further? Do you have any petrol . . . er, I mean gasoline with you? I'm afraid I've run out and that's why I've been stuck here. It was foolish of me, I know . . . '

It was as though the man hadn't heard her. He kept staring into her face. Unnerved, Donna stared back.

He swallowed past the cotton wool in this throat. 'Gasoline?' he asked in a strangled voice. 'You've run out of gasoline? Why didn't you say so before?'

'Well, I was getting round to it.'

Donna quelled her fear, deciding there was nothing for it but to accept any help he could offer or she'd be compelled to spend the night in the pickup. The alternative was to start walking; a most unattractive prospect since the sun was now getting ready to disappear behind the horizon.

'Do you or don't you?' she demanded when he didn't answer immediately. 'Have any petrol, I mean? I happen to be in rather a hurry.'

It sounded lame in view of the fact that she'd been doing nothing for hours on end, but the fact was she had no time to waste. 'I'm already late for my . . . for dinner.'

He frowned. 'You have a date

tonight?' To his utter amazement the thought annoyed him intensely.

But even more so was the fact that he'd felt compelled to ask. She could chase every last elderly moneybags in West Texas, for all he cared.

All he wanted was to remove himself from the woman's disturbing presence. If he wasn't careful he'd start becoming intrigued . . .

He said quickly, 'As it happens, I do have some spare gas in my vehicle. Hold it right there, Ma'am.'

A moment later he returned with a can and a funnel and made short work of filling her tank, obviously in a hurry to see the back of her.

Likewise! thought Donna.

She wound the window down further and reached for her purse. When he was finished she would be ready with some form of remuneration.

'I can't thank you enough, Mister . . . '

He did not supply his name, but kept staring at her as though wishing to imprint her face upon his memory.

Donna decided to ignore his lack of manners in view of the kindness he'd just shown.

She smiled tiredly. 'May I offer you something in return?' Hurriedly she tried to work out in dollars just how much the gasoline would have cost him.

The man reared back as though she'd just turned into a rattle snake. 'Thanking you kindly, Ma'am,' he grated, 'but I wouldn't take your services even if you came wrapped in chicken-fried steak seasoned with red onions and dripping with cream gravy.' The grey eyes snapped furiously beneath the black hat. 'Good day to you.'

Donna gasped. 'You are the most obnoxious, ill-mannered man I have ever met,' she yelled after him, 'and you have a mind like a sewer.'

He stopped in his tracks, his face a mask of cold anger. 'Yeah?'

Curiously, his eyes burned with a mixture of outrage, frustration and something else. Shame.

He'd just behaved like a buffoon, but

then Jared Jackson wasn't exactly known for his gallantry towards women, was he? Not since Merleen had left him seven years earlier for an aging rodeo champion.

'I'll run it by you one more time,' Donna told him roundly. 'You may think you're God's gift to the women of Texas, but where I come from no self-respecting female would look twice at a man with a shirt like that, even if it is Western style!'

His jaw dropped. 'Something wrong with my shirt?'

Donna sniffed. 'It's the most tasteless garment I have ever encountered. Allow me to point out that lime green and turquoise checks do not go well with a purple fringe.'

He looked thunderstruck. 'Is that so?'

'Most certainly. And while you're at it,' she advised severely, 'you can ditch that cloth thing you wear around your neck. Orange-red does not go with the rest of the ensemble.'

A decided gleam had replaced the

genuine astonishment in his eyes. 'I'm real sorry for offending your sensibilities, Ma'am,' he offered gravely, quelling the grin which threatened to turn him into a reasonable human being, 'but I happen to be colour-blind.'

He lifted his hat in a final salute. 'Good day, Ma'am.'

Donna watched his green Lincoln disappear into the distance and felt strangely exhilarated.

'Colour-blind,' she muttered wrathfully, 'that explains a lot!'

For some annoying reason that unexpected grin, coupled with the way he walked, had sent her heart hammering against her ribs. Which was very annoying because he was the rudest, most infuriating man she'd ever met.

2

Donna put her foot down hard on the accelerator in an effort to make up for lost time. She'd forgotten that darkness fell quickly in Texas, and by now the sun had almost set. In Ireland in summer, she thought with a small pang of homesickness, there'd always been the gloaming first . . .

She continued west, heading for the Texas hill country. The Double Circle Ranch which was situated north of Uvalde alongside the Frio River where they'd often bathed as children. It was with a sense of excitement and home-coming that she eventually turned off the road on to the dusty track leading to the log cabin.

Grandfather's fences, she noted in surprise, were in excellent order. Somehow she'd expected them to be dingy and broken down. The painted wooden gateposts and the sign bearing the two intertwined circles were exactly as she'd remembered them, but her grandfather's name was no longer displayed underneath.

It was no cabin which hove into view as she rounded the bend, but a long, low, white-painted, Mexican-style hacienda shaded by live oak trees and encircled by an expanse of tough, broad-leaved lawn. Lights showed behind some of its curtained windows, while the outside illumination revealed a neatly-paved area which led to a barn at the back of the house.

The barn, she noted in amazement, constituted part of a large complex comprising various other outbuildings and a big corral with a state-of-the-art stable block. The whole place looked prosperous, well maintained and impressive.

Donna caught her breath. Grandfather had certainly done very well for himself in the eight years since she'd seen him last, having demolished the original dwelling and replaced it with this imposing homestead which must have cost the earth.

She parked the Chevrolet pickup before the front door, climbed out wearily and turned her thoughts to dinner. It was almost eight o'clock and she was starving.

Grandfather would have eaten by now, of course; he always ate at six o'clock sharp and believed in the maxim 'early to bed, early to rise, makes a man healthy, wealthy and wise.'

Obviously after a little chat with Grandfather she'd have to find herself a meal in the kitchen and then take a long, cooling shower before climbing into bed in the little bedroom she remembered so well.

Tired but happy, she hauled her suitcase and the sack of groceries from the pickup and made her way to the massive front door. It was carved from sturdy oak with metal studs which gleamed dully in the light from the window to one side.

There was a large wrought iron knocker, too, but Donna decided not to use it. Instead, she turned the handle softly and pushed open the door. There was no need to knock. This was, after all, her home.

'Grandfather . . . ?' she called softly.

She deposited her heavy suitcase just inside the door and advanced into the hall where a tastefully-woven Mexican rug covered the terra-cotta floor tiles.

Yes, grandfather had certainly done well for himself. His taste had improved, too, she thought approvingly. The simple, rough pine had been replaced with sophisticated furniture of which even Seonaid would be proud.

A man came walking through the open-plan living area beyond the hall, his dark hair gleaming wetly from the shower he had just taken. He was tall and broad-shouldered, and clad only in a pair of clean jeans.

One or two drops of water still clung to his muscled chest as though he'd been in somewhat of a hurry. He looked up, saw her standing there and did a double-take.

Donna gazed back in shock, vaguely aware that something fierce had erupted from his stern mouth.

'Well, now, if it ain't little Miss Gasoline,' he drawled. 'What's it this time? Run out of money?'

Donna continued to stare, her eyes as wide as that of a calf which had just been roped and tied; acquiescent but half sick with apprehension.

'You're . . . you're the man in the green Lincoln!'

'Guilty as charged,' he drawled.

Her heart hammered sickeningly in her chest. After all the surprises she'd just received, another shock in the form of meeting Mr Macho Man in Grandfather's home was too much!

'Wh-what are you doing here, in the home of an ailing old man?'

'Old man . . . ?' His face hardened. 'So it's true, then. You really do go after old men with one boot in a pine box!

I'd say this one must have enough money to pay the Bill of Rights. What else would motivate a girl like you?'

'I beg your pardon?' she asked a little wildly.

He looked her up and down in and insolent manner, hiding the fact that her soft, open mouth and sweetly-pink lips had made his mouth go dry.

'Money,' he drawled with exaggerated patience. 'I'd say your boyfriend must be richer than the dirt in an old cow pen. That's why you're chasing him, isn't it? Sorry lady, but you've come to the wrong place. He ain't here.'

Donna had always considered herself to be a patient, good-tempered young woman but enough was enough, and she had had a very trying day.

'I am not listening to any more of your craziness,' she told him furiously. 'And you can stop staring at me like that! I am not in the mood for any more of your drivel, you insufferable man. I have no idea what you are doing here in

Grandfather's house, but I demand to know where he is.'

The inscrutable state became a blank one. 'Come again?'

Goaded beyond reasonable limits, Donna stepped forward and poked a pink-tipped finger at his massive chest.

'Well?' she demanded, past caring about impressive male attributes. 'Where is he?'

A variety of expressions fought for control over his face. 'Did you say . . . Grandfather . . . ?'

'I don't know who you are or why you are here in this house, but I haven't come all this way to be turned out. Where is he? Where is James McGuire?'

His jaw dropped. 'James McGuire? You're looking for James McGuire?'

He had no idea that the old man he so respected had become involved with a pretty little strumpet like this, even though she was young enough to be his granddaughter.

As far as he knew James had been a widower for many years and about as uninterested as they come in any other woman, but his late wife. And yet this female trouble-bundle was claiming to have a relationship with him.

He took a deep breath and stated clearly, 'James McGuire is not here.'

'Then where is he?'

He chewed his lip. Perhaps his old friend needed a little protecting here. This was one very determined and predatory young woman.

'He don't live here any more, Ma'am. He moved away.'

Donna gaped. 'Moved away? But that can't be so; he would have told me. I always write to this address.' She looked challengingly into his cold grey eyes. 'I believe you are lying.'

'No lies, lady, you got it straight from the mare's mouth. James McGuire moved away from this house, and that's a fact.'

'Then what is his current address?'

'I'm sure I can't help you, Ma'am.' The tones were implacable.

In a lithe movement he bent down to

retrieve her suitcase and the sack of groceries which were still standing at the front door. Good manners had dictated that he help her with her things.

'Wait!'

He shot her an irritated glance. 'Ma'am?'

'I will not be fobbed off like this! I'm not going anywhere until you tell me what I want to know. I want to know exactly where I can find my grandfather, James McGuire.' Her voice rose shrilly, 'and you will tell me now! This very minute!'

Slowly he replaced the suitcase on the floor and straightened to his full height of six feet four inches. 'Let me get this straight.' His voice sounded strangled. 'You are in actual fact the granddaughter of James McGuire?'

'I certainly am. I arrived from Ireland this morning.'

A dull red tinged his cheeks. He said slowly, 'then you must be Seonaid.'

'No. Donna-Marie,' she corrected.

He seemed dazed as he struggled to reassess his prejudices. 'You say you've come to visit your grandfather?'

'That is what I said.' Was the man dim as well as plumb crazy? 'And I haven't come all this way for nothing, sitting up all night in the aircraft next to an old man who snored, and then running out of pet . . . I mean gasoline on that beastly hot highway, only to find that Grandfather isn't here . . . ' she gulped, holding back sudden tears of frustration.

He looked at her as though he were seeing her for the first time. 'Dear, merciful heaven . . . '

If his sweet little grey-haired Grandmamma were here now she'd be twitching like a Mexican jumping bean. Yessir, he'd just made a prize fool of himself.

James had often spoken of his granddaughters back in Ireland, but he'd never mentioned how beautiful they were!

He cleared his throat and swallowed

twice. 'Would you . . . would you care to come into the living-room?'

Donna eyed him warily. 'I would prefer you to give me the directions to my grandfather's ranch, please, if, as you say, he has moved away. Just tell me where I may find him and I will leave you in the peace you so patently desire.'

Ouch. He deserved that! He hesitated. 'I'm sorry to have to tell you, Ms McGuire, that your grandfather really isn't here.' He took her gently by the arm and ushered her firmly into the living-room.

'Allow me to introduce myself, Ma'am. I'm Jared Jackson.' He indicated the brown leather sofa, 'please, take a seat. You'll have a cup of coffee first.' It was a statement, not a question.

Resignedly Donna nodded. She laid her still aching head on the backrest and closed her eyes. It had been a long, long day and it wasn't finished yet! She would drink her coffee, wring that blessed information out of him and then depart, never to set eyes on him again. Which suited her just fine!

'Why are you sleeping?' piped a voice at her elbow.

Donna sat up and blinked. 'What . . . ?'

'You're just like my Grandma,' stated the small person who was gazing solemnly into her face, 'she sleeps all the time.'

A child with huge grey eyes and untidy dark pigtails was standing beside her in a pink nightdress and matching fluffy slippers. Her arms were encased in numerous brightly-coloured plastic bangles and she bore an air of gleeful conspiracy. She hugged a battered teddy bear to her chest and took Donna's breath away by announcing triumphantly, 'you're my new Mamma, aren't you?'

'I . . . wh-what . . . ?'

'I've been asking God for a new mamma,' the little girl explained patiently. 'But Daddy says — '

'Daddy says go back to bed immediately,' a deep voice growled as Jared Jackson reappeared with a tray, having donned a black sweatshirt and a pair of soft leather moccasins in addition to the spotless jeans he'd first appeared in. He deposited the tray on the coffee table, placed a large hand on his daughter's shoulder and jerked his head in the direction of the passage.

'Off you go, Amy-Kate.'

'But Daddy, I want to talk to my new — '

'Bed!'

'Aw, all right, Daddy, I'm just going.' Ignoring her father's frown, she tossed a beatific smile in Donna's direction and promised, 'I'll see you soon.'

'Sorry about that,' her father apologised gruffly. 'I hope my daughter didn't embarrass you. She has a disconcerting habit of letting her tongue run away with her.' He gave a wry grin which caused Donna's heart to flip. 'Typical female!'

Being a kind girl, she hastened to reassure him. 'Oh, she didn't embarrass me at all. She's a real angel, isn't she?'

The strong lines of his face softened. 'She's a darlin', and she has me wrapped around her little finger, that's a fact. Like all women, she knows how to get her own way. Sugar?'

'Thank you.'

Donna stirred her coffee thoughtfully. His conversation was actually beginning to make some sense. Maybe after all there was a perfectly nice individual trying to get out from behind that stern exterior.

She gulped her coffee thankfully. Her thirst had seemed to be unquenchable since coming to Texas, which thought served to remind her of why she was here.

'My grandfather . . . ?' she prompted.

Jared laced his fingers around his mug and stared into its contents. 'I am sorry to have to tell you Miss McGuire that your grandfather is in the hospital in Uvalde.'

Donna went white. 'Oh, no! What happened?'

'He suffered cardiac arrest last week.

Fortunately we were in town together and I was able to get him to the doctor immediately.'

'Oh, the poor dear. What is the prognosis?'

Jared hesitated. 'He is holding his own, I believe. I visited him this afternoon and was just returning to the Double Circle when I passed you on the road. I had no idea who you really were, or I'd have . . . ' he broke off, filled with a kind of gut-wrenching shame at the memory. 'Accept my apologies, Ma'am. I . . . er . . . mistook you for someone else entirely.'

The truth was his late wife had left him a legacy of considerable mistrust. Just because she'd walked out on him, leaving him with a six-month-old baby before taking off, didn't mean that every woman he met had the same unfortunate tendencies.

Donna wasn't listening. She was far too concerned about her grandfather. She placed her empty mug on the table and stood up, still not quite able to understand why this man and his daughter were residing in what should have been her grandfather's house.

'I must go. I'll drive back to Uvalde and find a place to stay for the night and then I'll visit the hospital in the morning.'

He sprang up. 'No need. I'll let you have the key of your grandfather's cabin. You can stay there.'

'His cabin? I don't understand . . .'

'I bought the Double Circle Ranch from your grandfather a year ago. He had wanted to sell for some time, and as it happens I was looking for a place of my own.'

Donna stared at him, shocked. 'You bought this ranch from him?'

He inclined his head. 'Yes Ma'am.'

'Then . . . he no longer has a cattle ranch?' She was finding it extremely difficult to get her head around all this news.

'Oh, I wouldn't say that. He bought the neighbouring spread, a small place alongside the Frio River. After building the Double Circle into the prosperous place it is today he decided to retire and I can't blame him.

'He told me he had no family around who were interested enough to keep the place going after he'd gone so he built himself a cabin by the water, with a small bunkhouse for his hired hand, Hank Henderson.

'Your grandfather spends his days fishing and keeping a small herd of long-horned steers, and still rides old Beauty around the place helping to check on the fences between our two properties. It's about all he can manage these days.'

Donna's eyes lit with pleasure as she remembered the brown foal which had been born the last time she'd visited her grandfather. 'He still has Beauty? Oh, how marvellous. And Codger, the little black puppy?'

'Codger's around too, but he's an old dog now. Hank is taking care of him. I have to say that the poor critter's looking like his heart's as heavy as a bucket of hog livers. Missing your grandfather, obviously.'

Donna's tired brain digested all this information before she thanked him for the coffee and held out her hand. 'If I may have those keys now, Mr Jackson? I shan't keep you any longer.'

A sudden, unfamiliar pang of disappointment knifed through him. For some unearthly reason he wanted to delay her departure, and it annoyed him no end. He sprang up with what seemed to Donna to be unflattering alacrity.

'Sure thing, Ma'am. I'll drive you in the Lincoln.'

'Oh, but there's no need, I can find my own way.'

He was polite, but implacable. 'I'll drive you all the same, and have your own vehicle delivered to you first thing in the morning.' Something in his manner told Donna he was used to being obeyed, and she was too tired to argue.

'Well, all right, then. Thank you. But

what about your daughter? Will she be all right on her own?'

His glance was amused. 'My housekeeper, Mrs Gonzales, will keep an eye on Amy-Kate, no problem. Shall we go?'

They travelled for a few minutes before turning on to a small track which wound towards the river. At the end of it a long metal gate appeared, with a board attached. In the light from the headlights Donna read the words 'McGuire Ranch' and gave a heartfelt sigh of relief.

Once through the gate the road snaked between thick mesquite and cedar bushes until they arrived at a clearing on the hillside just above the water. In the middle of the clearing sat the dearest little cabin Donna had ever seen. Nearby was another small building, with a barn to one side, and a corral behind it. A 'mini' ranch, in fact.

'Oh, how perfect!' Donna breathed.

It was nowhere near as grand as Jared

Jackson's house but to her it was everything she could have wished for. It was home.

Within minutes Jared had turned on the lights, deposited her luggage in the spare bedroom and checked the entire house, followed from room to room by an overjoyed Codger.

'I believe Hank went into town for the evening,' he informed her, scribbling a number on the pad which lay on a table next to the telephone in the tiny hallway. 'Should you need assistance at any time, Ma'am, just give me a call. That's my home, and this here's my mobile telephone number.'

'I wish you wouldn't refer to me as Ma'am,' Donna blurted.

He cast a look of surprise. Amusement softened his stern mouth as he offered an explanation.

'We use the words 'Sir' and 'Ma'am' as a sign of respect here, so kindly refrain from mocking our Texas manners! We may be old-fashioned, but we like it that way. We still hold doors open for others, we offer our seats to old folks and we try to behave ourselves around our little old grandmothers. Our parents taught us that such things are expected of civilised people.'

'Oh, I didn't mean to ridicule you, it's just that 'Ma'am' makes me feel like an elderly spinster.'

He grinned. 'Rest assured that no man with his guitar tuned right would mistake you for his maiden aunt, Donna McGuire.'

She liked the way he said her name, and discovered that despite her earlier impressions, she really wanted to be friends with this intriguing man.

'Seeing we are to be close neighbours, you may continue to call me Donna,' she offered.

'Why, thank you, Donna. I'd be honoured if you'd call me Jared.'

They were treating each other with such polite friendliness that Donna had difficulty in believing he was the same man she'd encountered a few hours earlier.

She bestowed on him one of her beautiful smiles, and because she was grateful for the man's help and thankful at last to have found her grandfather's home, and because she was experiencing an uprush of fatigue-induced euphoria, she reached up and kissed him full on the mouth.

'Goodnight, then, Jared Jackson.'

He stared at her for a long moment before lifting his hat in an abrupt salute. 'Goodnight, Donna.'

Donna slept deeply and awoke as the sun was peeping over the hill. A soft whining reminded her of the presence of the little black dog beside the bed, who, when he'd seen her stir had placed his paw on the cover and licked her hand as though it were a rare treat. With a sleepy smile Donna snatched her hand away and leaned over to scratch his head.

'Sorry to take candy from a little dog, Codger, but it's time I was up and about.'

She flung back the covers and made for the small bathroom tucked away beyond the passage. After taking a shower she inspected her arms and shoulders in the mirror, pleased to find that the cream she'd hastily applied the night before had eased her sunburn considerably.

The soft pink skin was turning positively golden . . . a good omen for things to come. Soon she would be as brown as a berry.

Colour-wise, she mused, it would suit her dark hair and make her blue eyes all the more startling; a very satisfying thought. Without warning Jared Jackson's tanned face flashed into her mind, with his equally startling grey eyes and heart-stopping smile. It was another satisfying thought which she hastily brushed away.

Her new jeans looked rather stunning. She topped them with a sleeveless cotton blouse and slipped her feet into her new leather boots before fastening her shiny hair into a pony tail. After visiting her grandfather she would be ready for some good, hard work around the ranch.

The cabin, she noted in surprise, was fully air-conditioned and comfortable enough, but the heat outside would soon become unbearable. Well, she would simply have to get used to it!

Donna opened the back door and went to explore her surroundings while it was still relatively cool. She peeped into the barn with its straw bales and empty stalls, and then went to examine the bunkhouse which was neat and sparsely furnished with four bunk beds, a small kitchen and an ablution area to one side. The remains of someone's breakfast rested on the tough-hewn wooden table and at the sight she gave a small shudder. Beans and ham, congealing on the plate . . . ugh!

'Reckon you must be Mister David's lassie,' a gruff voice said behind her.

Donna swung around. 'Good morning. Yes, my father was David McGuire, son of James, and you must be Hank Henderson. Please don't think I was prying . . . '

The wizened old man who stood before her broke into wide grin. He looked about eighty and was dressed in grubby denim dungarees over a red checked shirt.

'Yes, Ma'am, I be Hank, at your service,' he informed her, touching his black cowboy hat with a gnarled finger. 'Reckon you must have arrived last night when I was in Uvalde. Welcome to the McGuire Ranch.'

'Thank you, Hank. Yes, Mister Jackson brought me here and told me all about my grandfather's illness, and I shall be visiting him today.'

Hank's grin disappeared. 'Sorry business, Missy.'

'Yes, but we must keep looking on the positive side. I'm sure he'll be home again soon,' Donna assured him. 'In the meantime I would ask you to carry on as usual, and you must allow me to help you.'

She glanced through the door at the barn which was showing obvious signs of neglect and could do with a fresh coat of paint. The fences too, were an unattractive, dingy white. She hadn't arrived a moment too soon, it seemed. Grandfather had always taken such pride in his surroundings but things were obviously getting beyond him. At his age it was perfectly understandable.

The elderly cowboy before her was shaking his head. 'This here ain't no life for a city-bred lass like you, Missy.'

Donna lifted her chin. 'I have always lived in the country, Hank. I had animals of my own, you know . . . a goat and hens and ducks. Besides, ranching's in my blood. I intend to remain here and when Grandfather's home again I shall help both of you.' At his look of doubt, she added with feminine wile, 'I'm a good cook.'

Hank brightened. 'That so?' He rubbed his chin. 'Reckon it'll be all right, then.' He hobbled off, whistling, to fetch Beauty from the corral where she was grazing peacefully with her companion, a neat black pony called Flint.

Donna set about the business of frying eggs and bacon in Grandfather's small kitchen. It opened on to the living area which possessed a small dining alcove at one end.

She and Codger shared the food and the little dog gulped it down as though he'd not eaten for days . . . a lie, of course, since Hank had obviously taken good care of him.

The animal then fixed her with an adoring eye and followed her about for the next hour as she unpacked her belongings, gave the furniture a once-over with a duster and swept the tiled floor.

At nine o'clock she refilled Codger's water bowl and made herself a mug of coffee, having unpacked the groceries she'd bought the previous day and finding space for them in the surprisingly well-stocked kitchen cupboards. Contrary to her expectations, her grandfather had his supplies well in hand.

It was time to contact Jared Jackson.

She had no idea what time visiting hours were at the hospital, but if need be she could be ready to leave immediately. Donna had just picked up the receiver and was dialling the number of Jared's mobile telephone when she heard a thump on the kitchen door.

'Donna?'

At the sound of Jared's deep voice Donna replaced the receiver, shocked at the way her heart was slamming against her ribcage. The truth was she was rather susceptible to deep, gravelly drawls, having fallen in love with a number of heroes from a variety of Western movies over the past few years.

Annoyed with herself for feeling attracted to a man she hardly knew and wasn't sure she even liked, Donna met him at the door with a fierce frown and a decided snap.

'What is it?'

He regarded her inscrutably from the doorway, every inch a cowboy in his regular working gear, his long legs encased in leather chaps and his broad shoulders straining against another one of those hideous shirts . . . without the red neck scarf, she noted in relief.

'Morning, Ma'am.'

'Oh . . . good morning,' Donna responded, glaring at the garment she found so offensive.

His eyes twinkled. 'Let me guess. The shirt?'

Donna rolled her eyes heavenwards. 'Some men never learn.'

He nodded happily. 'I guess not.'

'Shall we just say that your wardrobe needs a re-think?' She studied the shirt more closely, which was a mistake. It moulded his body in a way which set her heart hammering all over again.

'You offering to take on the job of re-thinker?' He sounded almost serious.

'Certainly not!' Dragging her eyes from the contemplation of his masculine beauty she said firmly, 'I intend to visit my grandfather as soon as possible this morning, so I would be grateful if I could have my — '

'Done.' He waved a gloved hand. 'Your pickup is standing out front under that live oak tree.'

'Oh. Thank you very much. Will you give me the directions to the hospital?'

'No need. I'm taking you there myself. Be ready in twenty minutes; that'll just give me enough time to clean up.' He walked off, whistling, to his Lincoln.

Donna took a deep breath. Of all the high-handed, bossy men! If this was an example of the take-charge, in-your-face Texas cattle baron, then she was in big trouble.

Nevertheless, she presented herself at the Double Circle ranch house in precisely twenty minutes, carefully made up, with her leather bag slung over her shoulder. It was heavier than usual since it contained four cans of Grandfather's favourite drink which had travelled all the way from Ireland in her hand luggage.

They reached the hospital where Jared explained that he had already made arrangements for her to see her grandfather, albeit briefly. Wordlessly he marched her into the elevator and rode with her to the second floor where he strode along the passage and stopped outside a particular door at which he knocked softly.

Her grandfather's weak, reedy voice told them to enter. At the sound Donna's throat constricted. She stood immobile until Jared laid a gentle hand on her back and propelled her forward.

'Mornin', Pardner,' he greeted the old man with affection, lifting his hat. 'I've brought little Miss Donna-Marie here to visit you for a few minutes. Mind you don't tire yourself, Sir.'

Grandfather, hooked up to innumerable tubes and devices and looking just as she'd remembered him only much more frail, folded his hands over the coverlet and peered at them from beneath a pair of white eyebrows every bit as bushy as his beard.

'Donna?' he asked incredulously. 'My little Donna-Marie? Is that really you?'

Donna flew into his arms. 'Oh, Grandfather, I have missed you so.'

The old man's voice turned gruff. 'Why didn't you come and visit? I bin waitin' on you, girl.'

'Have you really? Oh, if only I'd known . . . '

'You're a pretty lass, jes like your mother,' he told her, his weak voice filled with pride. 'And you have David's eyes.'

'Thank you. Seonaid's even prettier, though.'

His eyes grew thoughtful. 'You received my letter?'

'Oh, yes. That's why I'm here.'

'You here to stay, then, Donna? You'll bide a while and bunk down at the cabin?'

'Of course, Grandfather. I'll take over the housework and the cooking, if you like . . . ' And a lot more, only it might not be the time to say it. Grandfather, a feisty and independent man, needed to keep his self respect.

A warm glow filled the old man's

eyes. 'You'll stay as long as I say so, girl, and then you'll find a fine upstanding cowboy, like Jared here, and marry him. See if you don't.'

Donna flushed scarlet. 'I'll not have you matchmaking me, you scheming old thing,' she retorted fondly.

Jared cleared his throat. 'He needs to rest. We'll go now. You can visit again tomorrow.'

Donna, having forgotten that he was there, blushed again, peeping up at him from beneath her eyelashes. 'Please take no notice of what my grandfather has just said, Jared.'

They returned in silence to the car park where Jared helped her courteously into the passenger seat. Donna, still feeling awkward at the memory of her grandfather's words, felt compelled to clarify matters. It would not do at all if Mr Jackson thought she was thinking of taking her grandfather's advice.

'I can't see myself getting married for ages,' she declared loudly, 'least of all to a cowboy. I'm far too keen on a career.'

Jared sounded bored. ‘That so? Which career?’

Donna was ready with her answer. She’d been a part-time receptionist for old Doctor McCann at home, but had always been far more interested in having a few animals to care for.

‘Well, I like animals. I intend to run Grandfather’s ranch for him, even if it is only a few hundred acres. He’ll not be fit enough to do much when he comes out of hospital so it’s a good thing I’m here.’ After all, she stood to inherit the place.

Jared fired the engine. ‘How much do you know about ranching?’

‘Well . . . I kept a goat.’

He made a strangled sound in his throat and hastily turned it into a cough. ‘A goat,’ he repeated blandly. ‘I see.’

He eased the Lincoln out of its parking space.

‘Oh, she was no ordinary goat, to be sure.’ Donna explained. ‘Her name is Ermintrude, and I had two ducks,

Daisy and Loverduck, and a couple of hens who were quite good layers.'

Not a muscle of his face moved. 'Ducks and hens,' he repeated thoughtfully.

Encouraged by his interest, Donna quickly enlarged upon these matters, informing him of their daily habits, their diet and their sterling usefulness to mankind.

Jared drove the Lincoln smoothly out of the car park with a dead-pan face but beneath the mask he was falling even deeper in love.

Donna glanced at him suspiciously. His voice was non-committal and he wasn't smiling yet she formed the distinct impression that he was laughing into his leather boots.

He drew up before a long, low building on the outskirts of Uvalde and parked in the shade of a hackberry tree.

'May I dole out some good old cowboy advice?' he suggested in a carefully neutral voice. 'Stick to things you know about, Donna. Like . . . er, goats. Or bein' a doctor's receptionist. Ranching, even with a few animals, is a hard, full-time, round-the-clock job.'

'How did you know I worked in a doctor's surgery?'

'Oh, your grandfather has often spoke of his two talented granddaughters. It's a pity you haven't found the time to visit before now, when it may just be too late.'

He could have bitten out his tongue as soon as he'd spoken.

'What do you mean, too late?' Donna demanded.

'Well . . . ' His face gave nothing away as he sought for the right words. 'James is almost eighty,' he said reasonably, 'and one doesn't recover from an illness quite so quickly at that age.'

'He'll recover, I'll make sure of that,' Donna declared. 'With careful nursing he'll be just fine. I'm quite good at caring for people.' She looked around her. 'Why are we parked here?'

'It's lunch time and I'm hungry. I thought we'd have a meal and some iced tea before we head back. They make good chicken fried steak here.'

It was as they were finishing their lunch that the phone call came through from Mrs Gonzales.

Jared unclipped the mobile telephone from his leather belt and raised it to his ear. He listened for a moment in silence, looking grim. 'Thank you for letting me know,' he said quietly. 'Under the circumstances I doubt I'll be back in time to fetch Amy-Kate from school. Meet her for me, will you?'

He rang off, took a deep breath and clipped the instrument back on to his belt. 'Donna.'

She looked up. 'Yes?'

He leaned forward and took her hand. He'd never felt more like cherishing and protecting a woman than he did now, and how he hated to be the one to remove that sparkle from those extraordinary blue eyes.

At his touch a jolt of electricity went all the way up Donna's arm, but being a sensible girl, she ignored it. Why was it that the air seemed to bristle with energy every time they were together?

Her glance turned to one of puzzlement. 'What's the matter, Jared? You look . . . ill.'

Jared's grip tightened. 'Donna, honey,' he said quietly, 'I'm sorry to have to tell you that there has been some bad news.'

Donna sat up straight. 'B-bad news?' Her eyes turned very dark. 'It's not . . . concerning Grandfather?'

He nodded. 'That was my housekeeper to say that the hospital just telephoned.'

Donna's hand trembled beneath his like a little bird; small, wild and fragile. 'And?'

'James McGuire,' Jared said with compassion, 'has just passed away.'

3

Jared had never known anyone to look so colourless. Donna sat so still that she might have been a statue. Only her beautiful eyes appeared to be still alive, filled with shock and anguish.

She lifted a trembling hand to her mouth. 'No! It can't be . . . '

Jared summoned the waiter and quietly ordered a hot cup of tea. He spooned three sugars into the cup and stirred it.

In a daze, Donna gulped down the hot liquid. It brought a little colour to her cheeks and with it some coherent thought.

She lifted unhappy eyes to Jared's face. 'We'd better return to the hospital now. There'll be a great deal to attend to, won't there? I don't know much about these things . . . when we lost Mum and Dad, the solicitor handled it all, together with our minister from the church in the village. His wife was very kind. We stayed there for a week . . . '

Donna knew she was babbling but couldn't stop. 'Seonaid was seventeen and getting ready to go to university. I left school too, and that's when Doctor McCann offered me the job . . . '

Jared let her ramble and then assured her gently, 'There's no need for you to do anything. I'm taking you home to Mrs Gonzales.'

'What about the formalities?'

'I'll see to them.'

Donna took a deep, shuddering breath. 'How k-kind of you, but there's really no need. I'm older now and I can manage.'

He wasn't deceived by her too-quiet voice. She was in shock, yet her dignity and determined, hard-won calm elicited his admiration and respect.

'Of course you can. Nevertheless you will indulge me in this, Donna. I'm taking you to my housekeeper because I would not wish you be alone tonight. I hope you will stay in my home.'

To forestall her protests he added quickly, 'It would help me to know that someone will be with Amy-Kate this afternoon while I attend to your grandfather's matters.'

'You have a housekeeper,' Donna pointed out.

'Who will be busy, er, preparing the evening meal,' he improvised as he helped her to her feet. 'We'll go back to the cabin first so that you may collect what you need.'

Feeling dazed, Donna allowed herself to be helped into the front seat of the Lincoln. Jared leaned across and fastened her seatbelt, his face inches from her own. All at once Donna wanted to throw herself against his solid chest and cry out her anguish, but that would not do at all.

They drove some miles in silence before Jared said, 'Presumably you are still suffering from jet lag, Donna. It would probably be a good idea if you were to go to bed early. If need be Mrs

Gonzales will give you something to help you sleep . . . you'll feel much more like facing things in the morning.'

He was driving fast, his hands relaxed on the wheel, his face grave.

'Fine,' Donna agreed listlessly. The journey seemed endless. 'Are we nearly there?'

When they arrived at the Double Circle he ushered her into the living-room and seated her on the leather sofa. 'A cup of coffee,' he said briskly, and disappeared.

Donna took a deep breath, leaned back and closed her eyes. It was hard to believe that Grandfather was gone and would not be coming back to the cabin. She would now have to shoulder the responsibility for running his ranch, small though it was by Texan standards, and suddenly the prospect seemed daunting.

Being a resourceful girl, Donna thrust her doubts aside and told herself that she would make a success of it, no matter what. She had a lot to learn, but she would learn it. She had Texas in her blood, and that was enough.

A small, warm body snuggled up beside her. 'Are you sleeping again?'

Donna opened her eyes. Despite her inner turmoil she smiled. 'Hello, Amy-Kate. No, I'm not really sleeping. Grown-ups often close their eyes when they need to think.'

'Oh. What are you thinking about?'

Donna told her.

'But you won't have to look after Mr McGuire's cattle,' the little girl assured her confidently, 'my daddy will do that for you. He has plenty of ranch hands in the bunkhouse.' She added thoughtfully. 'When you're my mamma you'll be looking after me instead. You won't need to bother about the steers.'

Before Donna could think of a suitable reply Amy-Kate added blithely, 'Me, and all the other babies you and Daddy will have.'

'Amy-Kate!' Her father's growl was half groan. He placed a steaming mug into Donna's hands and turned to his small daughter in exasperation.

'You and I,' he told her sternly, 'need to have a little talk.'

Amy-Kate viewed her father with huge eyes. 'What about, Daddy?'

He frowned. 'About us. Honey, please understand that Miss McGuire is not your new mamma. She's our friend.'

'But friends can be mammas too,' the child insisted. 'Miss McGuire can be my mamma and my friend.'

Jared looked helplessly at Donna and cleared his throat. 'Sure, Honey, mammas are friends, but in this instance Miss McGuire is just our friend. Is that clear?'

Amy-Kate's small mouth turned down at the edges. A small tear squeezed itself from the corner of one eye. 'I guess.'

Donna, her cheeks pink, spoke quickly. 'When I was a small girl I had lots of dolls. There was Emma and Jemima and Sally, and Sally only had one eye but I loved her the best. When

I've had my coffee I'd like to see your dolls, Amy-Kate, so will you show them to me?'

Suitably diverted, the child slid off the sofa. 'OK, you can come to my room in a few minutes and I'll have my dollies for you. I have to dress them first.'

Be thankful for small mercies, Donna thought as Amy-Kate disappeared. At least the child hadn't called her 'Mamma'.

Jared let out a long breath. 'Once again, Donna,' he muttered stiffly. 'I apologise.'

At the earliest opportunity he would need to make it abundantly clear to his daughter that he had no intention whatever of providing her with a mother. End of story.

Despite her private grief the warmth in Donna's eyes made his heart turn over. 'No need, Jared. I understand where she's at. She's a dear little girl and she'll come round to the 'friendship only' bit after a little while, you'll see.'

He'd been burned by one woman and he didn't intend to open his heart to another.

His firm mouth compressed in frustration. Donna McGuire was one dangerous female. For his own sanity he would need to stay clear of her.

* * *

The funeral was held in the small cemetery just outside Uvalde. Donna was surprised to see how many people were there to pay their last respects to her grandfather, and it was very gratifying to discover how well-liked he'd been.

'Your grandfather was a fine man, Ma'am,' one young man told her as they turned away from the graveside. He gazed at her admiringly, but something else in his eyes made Donna slightly wary.

'I sold him that ranch a year ago, and a mighty fine piece of land it is, too, alongside the Frio River. Matter of fact,

I had my eye on it myself.'

He paused. 'I'm in real estate . . . Norton and Grey. We have our office in downtown Uvalde, East Main Street.'

He stuck out his hand and smiled charmingly.

'Name's Tyler Grey. I daresay you will be inheriting your grandfather's land?'

'Yes,' Donna murmured, hiding her distaste. 'If you'll excuse me, Mr Grey . . . '

She turned away, in no mood for chit chat with smooth young men in blue jeans and crisp Western shirts, even if their boots were made from the finest calf leather.

Jared Jackson was at her elbow. 'Ready to go, Donna? I've arranged a funeral tea at the Longhorn Hotel.'

'Oh, have you? Grandfather would have wanted a wake. That was thoughtful of you,' she told him gratefully. She would remember to ensure that he was reimbursed at a later date from

Grandfather's estate.

'No problem.' Then as though he wanted to put some distance between them he said mockingly, 'Always glad to help a neighbour. But don't count on this being a regular occurrence.'

Donna's chin lifted. 'Oh, you needn't imagine I'll be hanging on your coat tails, Jared.'

The man puzzled her. One moment he was being kind and solicitous, and the next moment hateful and mocking. She wasn't sure she liked him at all.

'Your grandfather's solicitor has been in touch with me,' he said suddenly, sounding distant. 'A Mr Joseph Ridley, from Kerrville. He asked me to let you know he'll be arriving later on this afternoon to read the will. He has asked me to be present as I held your grandfather's power of attorney, so I told him to come to the Double Circle at four-thirty. I hope you will find this arrangement suitable.'

Secretly annoyed that she hadn't

been consulted first, Donna nodded. 'Fine.'

Grandfather must have trusted Jared, but could she? They would get the formalities over and then she would go back to the cabin and cook dinner for herself and Hank. The poor old man had looked particularly lost at the funeral, which fact had wrung her heart. When she'd invited him to the cabin for steaks and mashed potato he'd almost wept.

'With onion gravy?' he'd asked hopefully.

'Onion gravy it is.'

When Donna finally got to bed that night it was well after midnight. She and Hank had drunk numerous cups of coffee as they'd pored over old photographs and talked about her grandfather, offering each other what comfort they could.

In the morning he arrived with a bunch of blue bonnets he'd picked in the field behind the house.

'Yer a good lass, Missy,' he informed

her, relieved that she had made it clear he would not be turned out of his home. 'It will be a pleasure to work for you, as it was for your grandfather. Sure as shootin' we'll take care o' the steers and the horses and make old James proud. Yessir.'

'I hope so,' Donna sighed, touched by his words. 'Thank you for the flowers, Hank.'

After lunch she settled down at the kitchen table to go over the ranch records and ponder her future strategy. Keeping the ranch going which would be a challenge to say the least, especially after what she'd heard yesterday from Joseph Ridley.

The solicitor had read the will in a dry-as-dust voice, informing her that James McGuire had left the property to his two granddaughters, Miss Donna-Marie McGuire and Miss Seonaid Hope-Jennings.

It came with two provisos, however. Firstly, should they wish to sell the property then his neighbour, Jared

Jackson, was to have the first option to purchase.

The second proviso was that should this happen within three months both girls were to receive a legacy of twenty thousand dollars each.

Donna had been speechless. It was almost as though the old man had wanted her to sell, and Jared to have the land! She took a deep breath and assured the solicitor that she and her sister had no intention whatever of selling.

'Seonaid is to give me her half share and I shall continue to live in Texas and run the McGuire Ranch,' she explained.

Both men had stared in open-mouthed astonishment.

'That's preposterous,' Jared grated.

'I would advise you to think again,' Mr Ridley told her sternly.

Donna shook her head. 'I have already given the matter a great deal of thought and my mind is quite made up. I will continue to operate my grandfather's business and that's that.'

'It hardly seems fair on Seonaid,' Jared pointed out.

Donna gave him a quelling look. 'My sister and I have an arrangement.' What it had to do with anyone else, she couldn't imagine. 'It is our own private affair.'

Jared's jaw hardened. His stare became cold enough to freeze the horns of a steer. 'I'll give you two months and you'll be ready to quit. And when you do, Donna McGuire, you'll come crawling to the Double Circle where I'll be waiting to sign that deed of sale. I'm more than ready to purchase your land; it'll give me that extra grazing I've been wanting . . . '

Donna gazed at the ranch records without seeing them. 'Stupid man,' she muttered, remembering Jared's threat. 'I'll show him!'

Brave words, and well she knew it. James McGuire, expecting his granddaughters to sell the place immediately, had not left enough capital to ensure its maintenance. Instead, he'd endowed various charities and numerous old friends, not forgetting his faithful ranch hand, Hank.

Not that she begrudged anyone a legacy. It was just that she would now be forced to use her own meagre savings to keep the ranch viable and when these ran out, as they would do pretty soon, she would be forced to apply to one of the banks in Uvalde for a loan. There was no other way to keep the operation afloat.

Donna sighed. If only her grandfather had known how she felt about ranching! All she needed now was the chance to prove herself. With Hank's help and advice she was determined to make a success of everything. Naturally it required hard work, but she had never been afraid of hard work.

She would build up the beef herd and try to get some good market prices at the stock yards in Fort Worth next season. That way the McGuire Ranch would stay in business and go from strength to strength.

As for her enigmatic, grim-faced neighbour, Jared Jackson, he could give her as many icy stares as he wanted, it made no difference.

* * *

Donna was up before dawn the next morning. As usual she pulled on her working gear of denims, cotton blouse and boots, and went into the kitchen for an early-morning cup of coffee while she pondered what to make for breakfast.

Hank arrived shortly afterwards, his wrinkled old nose sniffing the air appreciatively. 'Sure is good to have you takin' charge o' the meals, Missy,' he told her, easing his scrawny, arthritic body down on to a kitchen chair and tucking his table napkin under his chin. 'Reminds me of when my Betty-Lou was alive.'

As they munched their sausages and French toast Donna outlined the tasks ahead. 'I'd like to check the feed situation with you, Hank. According to Grandfather's records we need to re-order supplies pretty soon. I'll drive in to Uvalde to the feed and tack store where he had an account and speak to the manager. Will you let me know what other supplies we need? Like veterinary requirements? You will have to help me along a little. I'm not sure how often the cattle are dipped, and there'll be the deworming of the calves . . . '

She broke off, suddenly appalled at the amount she still had to learn about ranching. There would be haymaking and the new calves to be branded as well.

'Sure thing, Missy,' Hank assured her confidently. 'You just leave it to ole' Hank. I bin at this game a long time.'

Donna gave him a relieved smile. 'While I'm in town I'll buy some paint for the barn,' she promised, and went to wash the dishes.

The heat was building up in the cab as she rode into Uvalde. She had returned the blue Chevrolet to the hire company and was now using her grandfather's shiny black Dodge Ram pickup, a vehicle she'd been relieved to find in excellent order, standing in the large garage next to Hank's noisy red rattletrap.

Donna found a parking space in the main street and went about her business with purpose and determination. At the feed store she introduced herself with a confident smile and assured the manager she would continue in her grandfather's footsteps . . . if he would allow her the same credit . . . ?

He eyed her doubtfully. 'I'll let you know. Ain't no job for a woman, ranching, if you'll pardon my saying so, Ma'am.'

Donna had ended up writing a personal cheque which further depleted her savings. When the supplies were safely stowed, she went in search of a drug store for some toiletries and then a supermarket for fresh eggs.

When this chore was accomplished she found a hardware store and spent half an hour having the paint mixed to her exact requirements.

Donna glanced at her watch, astounded to see that it was almost one o'clock. She spotted a diner nearby and decided to have lunch before heading back to the ranch. She chose a booth away from the window so that she could avoid the bright sunshine streaming through it. Even with the air conditioning on it was warm.

'Hi. I'm Lacey McCoy,' a smiling young waitress in a pink uniform introduced herself. She gave Donna the friendly once-over. 'You're new in town, aren't you?'

'Yes. Donna McGuire. I've just arrived from Ireland.'

'I know. You're old James McGuire's granddaughter. Sorry to hear about his death, honey. We'll miss him. He was a regular of ours.' She took out her order pad and added chattily, 'Heard you're staying on at the McGuire Ranch.'

'Yes, I am.' News here, thought Donna, travelled almost as fast as in the village back home.

Lacey viewed her curiously. 'Well, I wish you luck. If you need any help you can always consult that sexy neighbour of yours, Jared Jackson. He's a real trouper. Helped me once with my car when I ran out of gasoline, and then wouldn't take any money for it.'

I'll bet, Donna thought sourly.

The waitress reached for the pencil behind her ear. 'What'll you have, Donna?' She gave a grin. 'This is small-town Texas. We're not Dallas or Houston so it's no good asking for filet mignon or pasta primavera 'cause we only do burgers, fried chicken and grilled steak. With mashed potato, of course. And salad, or soup, if you'd prefer it.' She handed Donna the menu card. 'You take it easy now, I'll be right back.'

Donna glared so fiercely at the menu card that her eyes began to ache.

A deep male voice beside her made her start. 'Good day, Ma'am, may I join you?'

warily. 'Oh, it's

smiled engagingly.
Donna? I'd sure
ld buy you lunch
tty little lady like
dining alone. No

may. She didn't
Grey with his
eminded her of
same beguiling
ed a ruthless,
grasping disposition. When crossed, he would turn positively nasty. Being True Blue herself, she could smell a phoney a mile away.

She was deliberating about his offer when she caught sight of Jared Jackson glowering at her from his seat near the window. If the set of his mouth was anything to go by he was as little pleased to see her as she was to see him.

Donna lifted her chin defiantly and favoured Tyler Grey with one of her brightest smiles. She hadn't meant to encourage him quite so warmly, but Jared's uncalled-for hostility had angered her.

'Well . . . thank you, Tyler.'

She waited for him to be seated before peeping at Jared again from under her eyelashes. It was just as she expected: those grey eyes were still shooting bullets. Mortified that he had noticed the peep, she went faintly pink.

Jared regarded her for a long moment, his face carefully blank, then he lifted his hat in polite acknowledgement and settled it firmly back on his dark head before turning pointedly away in order to study the menu.

Donna's appetite, so sharp a moment ago, now quite deserted her. Nevertheless she was determined not to allow the man to spoil her day, and chose chicken, salad, and French fries.

'Iced tea or water?' asked Lacy, tucking her pencil back behind her ear.

'Water, thank you.' Donna didn't care over much for iced tea, preferring a nice hot cuppa instead.

Tyler Grey was warmly attentive. 'I've heard you're staying on at the McGuire Ranch.'

He appeared to be particularly interested when she described her future plans and led her on with skilful questions. It was only afterwards that Donna realised she'd told him much more than she'd intended, and had learned almost nothing about Mr Grey himself.

'There's a town social on Saturday evening . . . a barbecue, a little dancing, a little music. The Texas Tornadoes will be playing, Donna. Care to come?' Tyler invited. 'It should be good. I'd be honoured to accompany you.'

She was keen to make new friends and establish herself in the community, and what better way than to begin by socialising?

'I'd like that, Tyler,' she nodded.

'Great. I'll call for you at five o'clock.'

'Oh, please don't bother; I prefer to drive myself. It's only a twenty-minute journey.' That way, if she wanted to leave early she could.

The last thing a girl needed when out with a relatively strange man was to feel like Davey Crockett, holed up in the Alamo.

Tyler shrugged. 'Suits me. I'll meet you there.' He explained where to find the large gardens and added in an offhand voice Donna didn't much care for, 'Wear something pretty, will you? I can't abide girls with no dress sense. I intend to show you off.'

'Should I be flattered?' Donna muttered sweetly as Tyler called for the bill.

They left the diner together, passing Jared Jackson's table on the way out. His grey-eyed gaze was filled with such mockery that Donna defiantly favoured him with a sweet smile. It turned his face to stone.

Beneath the stone, Jared Jackson was fuming in frustration. Darned woman knew how to yank his chain, all right! She had no more sense than a corn cob. Everyone in town knew that Tyler Grey was trouble. The man was as slippery as a greased pig.

The man in question walked thoughtfully back to his office as he pondered his next move. He'd already paid the tack and feed store a visit to warn them, but perhaps he'd call in there again tomorrow . . .

* * *

Donna returned to the pick-up and quickly headed out of town, driving to the sounds of country music being played over the car radio.

The heat inside the cab was barely under control. The sooner she reached the ranch the better. Black always absorbed the heat and unfortunately she hadn't been around to advise her grandfather when he'd purchased the Dodge. Men!

On reaching the ranch Donna enlisted Hank's help in unloading the supplies. She watched worriedly out of the corner of her eye as the old man struggled to manhandle the heavy sacks into the barn. At this rate she would be forced to hire another ranch hand, an expense they didn't need just at this moment.

She stowed the new paint in one of the sheds, together with the brushes and rollers. It would be quite an effort to paint the barn, but there was a reliable extension ladder she could use. She couldn't wait to get started in the morning.

Two days and much hard labour later, Donna stretched her aching back and viewed her handiwork with satisfaction. She tossed the paint brush into a bucket and headed towards the cabin for a well-deserved cup of tea.

The kettle had just boiled when a vehicle screeched to a halt outside her back door. To her dismay, Donna recognised it as the green Lincoln.

'What,' Jared demanded in a strangled voice, 'is that . . . ?'

Donna gave him an icy stare. 'Good afternoon to you, too. What is what?'

He pointed wrathfully. 'That!'

'Oh, that? It's a barn.'

'Wrong. It's a purple barn!'

'Lilac,' she corrected hotly. 'It's the latest shade in chic. Anyway, I thought you were colour-blind.'

'I am, with certain colours . . . I confuse greens, reds and browns, and it's called 'red-green colour-blindness'. But lilac . . . '

He shook his head in disbelief. 'Man, but you Irish have some quaint little ways.'

Despite herself Donna grinned. 'Wait until you see my fences. I'm painting them lilac and lemon. Lilac for the uprights and lemon for the horizontals.'

Jared's jaw dropped. 'Now look here, this is a ranch, not a circus.' When he acquired the McGuire Ranch he'd be forced to re-paint everything, he reflected in annoyance.

'There's nothing wrong with colour, mister, it brightens the world.'

'That's a bunch of malarkey,' he muttered darkly.

His gaze suddenly encountered a

plate standing on the counter. His eyes brightened. 'Is that a pie?'

'It is. Lemon meringue pie,' Donna told him pointedly.

'Huh. Thought so.'

She took pity on him. He didn't have a mean and hungry look, exactly . . . just a certain small-boy hopefulness. 'The kettle has just boiled. Will you join me for some tea and pie? I made it early this morning.'

'Coffee, if I may.'

Donna hid a smile. Suddenly it felt good to be on a friendly footing again. 'It's a deal, cowboy. Sit down.'

Jared lowered his considerable stature on to a kitchen chair and frowned. He couldn't believe he was doing this. He'd come here to discuss what was to be done with James McGuire's leaking galvanised stock tank which he'd just finished welding, and here he was sitting in the woman's kitchen practically begging to sample her cooking. He must have a death wish.

He cleared his throat. 'Your grandfather's tank. Where do you want it dumped?'

Donna's mouth dropped open. He was talking in riddles again, just when she had decided he was normal.

'Er . . . tank?'

'Sure. Where shall I put it?'

At her look of complete bewilderment, he explained as though to a two-year-old. 'The tank for your cattle, Donna. You'll have to tell me where to drop it off tomorrow. It's a mighty big piece of furniture, and I'm a busy man.'

Donna reached for the instant coffee she'd had the foresight to buy that morning. 'I . . . see.'

He laughed. 'No, you don't. You'll never make a rancher, take it from me.'

'That's where you're wrong, mister. Anyway, what do the cattle need a tank for? They're not in the army.'

'Ma'am, I'm talkin' about a water tank.'

'Oh.' Donna felt about two inches high. How was she to have known?

'We sometimes use these things as a swimming hole, as well,' he explained kindly. 'When the men are out checking fences and the heat gets too much, they simply take off their clothes and jump in. Keeps them sane.'

Carefully Donna sliced a large piece of pie. As she plopped the pie onto his plate she decided it would be a good thing if he choked on it. The man was a constant threat to her peace of mind.

'You can return the tank to the same place you took it from,' she informed him. 'Wherever my grandfather was using it will be OK by me.'

'The north pasture? Fine.' He took a huge bite and savoured it as though it was angels' food. 'Mmm, this sure is good.'

'Thank you.'

'There's a social evening in town on Saturday,' he mentioned casually.

'Yes, I know. I'm going with Tyler Grey.'

For some reason Jared felt like throwing up. No reflection on the pie.

'Tyler Grey,' he growled, 'is not to be trusted. Be warned.'

Donna looked down her straight little nose. 'I am well able to take care of myself, Jared.'

'Sure you are,' he jeered. 'Any lady who paints her barn purple can spot a jerk a mile off. It's obvious you think you know more about men than a white-faced calf knows about sucking.'

'Lilac, not purple,' corrected Donna coldly. 'And I'll thank you to keep your opinions to yourself. If you're going to make rude comments you can leave my kitchen and take your pie with you!'

Unhurriedly Jared savoured his last mouthful before swallowing it. Slowly he pulled out his handkerchief and wiped his fingers.

'Sure thing, Ma'am.' His eyes glinted with laughter as he unfolded his large frame from the chair. 'That,' he told her, 'was delicious. Thank you. I enjoyed the coffee, and I enjoyed the lilac pie, too.'

'Lemon!' Donna yelled.

'Whatever.'

He sauntered from the kitchen and heaved himself into the Lincoln, rolled down the window and gave her a large wink.

'Enjoy yourself with the jerk on Saturday night, sweetheart.'

'That,' gritted Donna through her even, pearly white teeth, 'will be no problem at all.'

As Jared drove up the hill his smile turned bitter. As usual when around Ms Donna-Marie McGuire he had acted like a complete idiot.

Despite her fabulous cooking the woman brought out the worst in him, no kidding. And now the little darlin' was determined to hitch her wagon to that of Mr Tyler Grey, unscrupulous swine who was known to be on the make, especially when it came to females he imagined had a buck or two.

He'd been planning to watch a movie on Saturday night, but it looked as though he'd be required for duty instead.

He'd be forced to go to that social in

order to keep a stern eye on little Miss Gasoline here. She was the most headstrong, crazy, adorable woman he'd ever encountered . . . and a woman he was more than ever determined to stay away from. So how come he was giving up his whole evening to play babysitter?

Jared drove the Lincoln into the garage and cut the engine.

He was doing this, he told himself firmly, because he owed it to his old friend, James, that's why. It had nothing whatever to do with the way James's granddaughter pushed his buttons.

He let himself into the house, wondering what Mrs Gonzales had in mind for their dinner that evening. He hung up his hat on a peg in the scullery and went to wash his hands.

The fact of the matter was that despite all his good intentions and despite all the pain she was likely to cause him in the future, he would never be able to let Ms Donna-Marie McGuire out of his life.

4

By lunch time the following day Donna had completed painting the fence around the corral. She stood back to admire her handiwork just as Hank arrived for his midday meal.

'Doesn't colour make a wonderful difference, Hank?'

Hank stared in puzzlement at the lilac and lemon stripes, his eyes screwed up against the sun. 'Uh . . . sure is pretty, Missy. Reminds me o' the funfair at San Antonio when I was a boy.' And with that Donna had to be content.

At that moment, Jared drew up in a large cream pickup to inform her that he and one of his ranch hands had just deposited the water tank in the north pasture.

'There's a water faucet nearby. You can run a hose and fill it up anytime.'

Donna thanked him politely and

waited for him to comment about the fence. She watched hopefully as he put his head through the window and viewed it for a long moment in silence.

'Well?' she demanded.

'It'll make those horses of yours sea-sick. You sure are one crazy woman, do you know that?'

He fired the engine. 'If you wish to waste precious time on fripperies instead of doin' some real work, that's your lookout. Complete waste of time and effort if you ask me, besides the cost of the paint. I'll only have to get it whitewashed again when I take over your property. Good day, Ma'am.'

Donna stared after him, speechless.

Behind her, Hank gave a small cough. 'It's lunch time, Missy.'

Donna hurried inside to dish up the left-over Irish stew, her anger evident as she slammed the plates on to the table and clattered the saucepan into the sink.

* * *

For the next two days she worked extremely hard at being a hands-on rancher, doing 'real work', as Jared would have called it. Even to herself she would not admit that she held the unconscious hope that he would arrive and catch her in the act, which, naturally, did not happen.

In the process, however, Donna learned a lot. She learned to feed an orphaned bull calf, get it dosed and tagged and castrated, and then fenced in.

She helped Hank build the enclosure near the cabin where she could give it regular meals, resigned to the fact that its hungry bellows would have to be endured day and night for the next few weeks.

'The calf's name is Norman,' she informed Codger, who sniffed disdainfully at the new arrival before loping inside for his dog biscuits.

Saturday arrived all too soon. Donna combed through her meagre wardrobe and decided she would have to drive into Uvalde to look for a new outfit for the social that evening. Her clothing was mostly working gear, with one or two skirts which had seen better days.

Being a colour-conscious girl, she knew exactly what she wanted, and found it in a small ladies' boutique with the unlikely name of 'Wanda's Wear For Women'.

She chose an eye-catching skirt in pale blue velvet with a matching cowgirl-style bolero trimmed with embroidered bluebonnets the exact colour of her eyes.

She slipped into the diner for a quick drink before heading home, and was welcomed like an old friend by Lacey McCoy.

'Goin' to the social tonight, Donna?' she asked chattily.

Donna nodded. 'Tyler Grey asked me. Are you going?'

'Sure.' Lacey's eyes lit with excitement. 'Bobby Ray has asked me. He works in the bank, you'll meet him tonight. It's early days yet, but if things work between us maybe I'll become

Mrs Bobby Ray Jones. I'd give anything to be able to stay at home and have lots of babies. I always wanted a big family, but that's maybe because I grew up kinda lonely myself. What'll you be having?'

Donna placed her order, waited for it to arrive and made short work of the tall lime soda. Since arriving in Texas she had never ceased to be thirsty.

''Bye, honey,' Lacey mouthed as Donna left the diner. Lacy seemed a sweet girl and Donna was pleased to find that she'd made at least one friend in Uvalde.

She hurried back to the Dodge which had been parked under a tree behind the diner, only to discover that the air in all four tyres had been removed. A chalked message was scribbled across the windscreen:

You're not wanted in Uvalde. Go home.

Shocked, Donna stood and stared. Who would do a thing like this? She wasn't aware of having made any enemies . . . unless it had been Jared, who must want to buy her land pretty badly . . .

She arrived home an hour later after having been assisted by a man from the service station on the corner, and flounced into the kitchen to feed Codger and the calf. A ham salad would have to be made for Hank, too, and left on the kitchen counter for him to find later.

When Donna finally took a shower and put on her new clothes she felt a lot better. Her soft leather boots were just right with the outfit and the tiny silver and blue studs she'd bought were the exact colour of her eyes. Although she wasn't a vain girl she couldn't prevent a feeling of pleased satisfaction.

'Very nice,' Tyler told her as he took her arm in what Donna felt was an unnecessarily proprietary manner.

'Thank you, Tyler.' She couldn't say the same for him, taking an instant dislike to the too-tight jeans, the loud shirt and the alligator cowboy boots which were polished to such a high gloss she could almost see his face in them.

Tyler led her to one of the tables near the barbecue where they selected their meat and placed it on the metal grids over ten-gallon drums which constituted the cooking arrangements. Once their steaks were sizzling, he offered her a glass of beer.

Donna refused politely. She was not partial to beer. 'I'll have orange juice, if I may.'

For a moment Tyler's smooth charm slipped. His tones held a faint sneer. 'Orange juice? Isn't that a little juvenile?'

He had no intention of letting Donna off so lightly, and intended to lace her orange juice with a little gin.

'You heard the lady,' Jared's voice cut in curtly. 'Orange juice, it is!'

Tyler swung around. 'I'll thank you to keep out of this, Jackson,' he said belligerently.

'Oh, yeah?' Jared took a step closer, his face grim.

Donna looked from one to the other, wide-eyed. One dogfight coming up! What was it with men?

Jared hooked his thumbs into his leather belt and continued to give Tyler a quelling look. The other man backed down suddenly with a mumbled, 'I'll get the drinks', and disappeared.

'Thank you for nothing,' Donna rounded on Jared coldly.

He looked at her inscrutably. His grey eyes held a decided glint and his voice was pure silk. 'Evening, Donna-Marie. May I say that you look like a million dollars?'

Donna batted her eyelids in exaggerated coyness. 'Why, thank you Mr Jackson. May I say that you do, too? No loud shirt, for once.'

He smothered a grin. 'Why, how kind of you, Ma'am. Shall we dance?'

'Certainly not. The band hasn't even started up yet.'

Jared looked around in surprise. 'It hasn't? That's too bad. Later, then.'

Tyler reappeared with Donna's drink

of pure orange juice. He tossed Jared a defiant look which said, 'get lost'. Jared ignored it completely. He was here to keep an eye on little Donna McGuire, and keep an eye on her he would! For old James's sake, of course.

'Jared! Hello darlin', where have you been hiding?' a nasal female voice broke into the fizzing tension which had settled in the air. Its owner was a shapely blonde in a too-tight skirt and numerous gold bracelets which jangled as she attached herself to Jared's arm.

She smiled up at him adoringly, her coy manner hiding a ruthless determination. 'Honey, why haven't you returned my calls?'

'Well, there you are, Bonny-Sue.' Jared greeted her blandly, his amused eyes on Donna's outraged face. 'May I introduce everyone? This here's Tyler Grey and he's escorting this pretty lady, Miss Donna McGuire . . . Miss Bonny-Sue Simpson. Bonny-Sue,' he told them with just the right amount of casualness, 'is heir to her father's ranch, The

Silver Buckle. Fifty thousand acres of prime land near Fredericksburg.'

Tyler's eyebrows rose. 'Well, now, that is mighty interesting.'

'Isn't it?' Jared agreed, disentangling himself from Bonny-Sue's clutches and suggesting that he might help her choose her meat. He lifted his hat at Donna, gave Tyler a curt nod and turned away with Miss Simpson in happy tow.

Later that evening when Donna was in bed she chided herself for feeling jealous of Bonny-Sue Simpson. She considered that the predatory woman had made an unseemly play for Jared's attentions all evening.

On the one occasion that Jared had asked her to dance, Bonny-Sue had kept a sharp, assessing eye on the pair of them so that Donna had begun to feel downright uncomfortable.

She'd been forced to look up into his face instead; anywhere rather than at the confounded woman. What she'd seen in Jared's eyes had set her pulses racing.

It confused her, to say the least. I mean, why would a man who'd let the air out of her tyres look at her as though she was a luscious dessert?

Her thoughts turned from Jared to Tyler Grey. She hadn't much cared for the way he'd fished for information concerning her financial position. She'd been deliberately vague, refusing to divulge a thing, with the result that he'd become petulant, hiding it beneath repeated offers of help should she wish to sell her land, and broad hints about a friend who would be willing to purchase it.

Out of sheer curiosity Donna had asked what the land was worth in commercial terms.

'Oh, I wouldn't pay more than two dollars an acre,' he'd told her in a know-all voice, 'plus a few thousand for the buildings. The land's rather hilly. Most ranchers prefer flat country.'

'Which is just as well, isn't it?' she'd said sweetly, 'because I'm not selling.'

Two thousand dollars for the land

sounded very little to her, but Tyler was a real estate agent and he was bound to know current market prices.

Just how hilly the land was, was borne out to her the following week when she and Hank rode around the entire boundary to inspect the fences. At the end of the weary, heat-filled day Donna slipped off Flint's back and discovered that her legs had turned to jelly.

She had never before in her life spent an entire day in the saddle and the experience left her feeling decidedly wobbly. Donna McGuire, she told herself severely, would have to toughen up!

Hank was sympathetic. 'I'll see to the grooming, Missy. You go and take a hot bath.' He spat tobacco juice on to the ground, took the bridle from her unresisting hands and went off muttering, 'ain't no job for a woman, ridin' fences . . . '

Still feeling stiff the following morning, Donna managed to fill the feeding bottle with milk and hobble out to the pen to give Norman his breakfast. She'd been waking up at four o'clock every morning in order to give him his early feed, and anyone would think by his desperate bellowing that she was a neglectful mother! The truth was that Norman couldn't get enough.

Donna grinned as the calf devoured his food. Perhaps Jared's little daughter would like to give him his bottle one afternoon, she thought, making a mental note to ask if she could fetch Amy-Kate after school. It must be lonely for her out on the ranch with no playmates.

She made herself a mug of coffee and hauled out the bacon and eggs from the refrigerator. Thankful that her grandfather had left plenty of extra bread in the freezer, she took out a loaf and popped a few slices into the toaster.

After breakfast she was determined to force herself back on to the black pony. It was the quickest way to loosen up again, Hank had told her.

Donna made her bed, tidied the cabin and piled a load of laundry into the washer before fastening her hair into a long plait to keep it from falling across her face as she rode.

She hobbled out to the barn where Hank had just finished cleaning the stables with a pressure washer, having already let the horses into the corral. She watched as he hefted a bale of hay from the storage and felt in his pocket for his Swiss army knife in order to cut the rope which bound it.

'Nice morning,' he said laconically as he began to spread the straw around with a pitchfork.

'Beautiful.' Donna sighed. 'The colours at sunrise were spectacular, did you notice? All fiery orange turning to pink and gold.'

'Colours again . . . ' growled Jared from behind. 'You are allowed to think of other things, you know. Like good, honest hard work.'

Donna spun around, incensed. 'There is nothing wrong with admiring God's handiwork,' she snapped.

'Sure, but not at the expense of your chores.'

'Who said I was neglecting my chores? I'll have you know I've been up since four, and I have never been afraid of hard work.' She added forthrightly, 'you are an impossible man!'

His mouth twitched. 'Four? Doing what?'

Donna reeled off her activities. 'And I don't know why I'm telling you all this because it's none of your business.'

His voice turned silky. 'Oh, but it is, Donna. I'm protecting my interests. When I take over your property I would like to know that it has been adequately maintained.'

Donna pointed to the barn door. 'You may take yourself off now, Mr Jackson,' she said sweetly. 'You are wasting my valuable time with your drivel. I would like to get on with those oh-so-pressing chores! Good morning.'

She ignored his chuckle and turned smartly on her heel, only to spoil her grand exit by her ungainly hobble.

Jared was at her side in two seconds, his eyes concerned. 'You've hurt yourself. What happened, Donna?'

'I am perfectly fine, I'm just a little stiff, that's all.'

'Why are you stiff?'

Her eyes flashed. 'I am not used to spending an entire day in the saddle, as I did yesterday. And I would thank you not to laugh!'

For once Jared's eyes held no mockery, only a lingering tenderness. 'Am I laughing?' he asked gravely. Unable to help himself, he placed his hands on her shoulders and dropped a kiss on her surprised mouth. 'You're a plucky girl.'

A spark of some emotion sizzled up Donna's spine, and she tamped it down with all her might; only it wouldn't be tamped. She gazed into Jared's eyes with a puzzled look, as though examining his face for clues.

She'd had kisses before, but none had ever left her feeling this way . . . as though Jared Jackson had slipped past her long-held defences and was about to capture her heart. Which was ridiculous!

Jared, far from immune to that kiss, was telling himself sternly to get a grip. He snatched his hands from Donna's shoulders and wrenched his gaze away.

'Those chores,' he reminded her shortly.

'All in good time.' She raised her eyebrows at him. 'Why did you come?'

Jared slapped his hand against his forehead. 'I forgot . . . I've come to . . . invite you to dinner this evening. Six o'clock. Amy-Kate has been asking to see you.' At her look of doubt, he added quickly, 'Mrs Gonzales would be very disappointed if you refuse. She's about to embark on a new recipe for steak pie.'

Donna cast about in her mind for an excuse, but could find none. Besides, a small part of her wanted to go, very much. It was a puzzling thing, but despite her dislike of the man, Jared was turning into someone rather important to her.

Some imp of mischief seized her tongue. 'Why don't you ask Bonny-Sue instead? I'm sure she'd be only too delighted. She's waiting for your call, remember?'

Jared's face closed. 'It's you my daughter wants to see, Donna, not Bonny-Sue. Amy-Kate said something about clothing for her Barbie dolls.' That much was true, anyway.

'Then on that basis, I accept.' She looked pointedly at her watch. 'You will have to excuse me.'

'Of course.' Politeness itself, Jared lifted his hat. 'Good day, Ma'am.'

Donna went back into the barn for her tack, took it out to the corral and saddled Flint. Beauty, her grandfather's mare, came running up expectantly.

'Hello, sweetheart,' Donna greeted the elderly animal, 'Hank will fetch you later. That's a promise.'

She spent the next hour riding up the hill to the north pasture where she inspected the water tank Hank had already filled. The sparkling water did indeed look inviting but she would not allow herself to be tempted. The pasture bordered Jared's land and his men were always about.

By five o'clock, Donna had fed both Codger and Norman and put away the laundry. She dished up the beans and sausages she'd made for Hank's supper and went to take a shower before donning her new blue skirt, matching it with one of the blouses she'd bought in Fort Worth on the morning she'd arrived.

Because it was still hot she pinned her thick hair into a simple knot, leaving one or two artful wisps about her face. Her skin, she noted with pleasure, was now nicely tanned and showed to perfection the silver cross and chain about her neck; a gift from her father before he'd died.

Feeling warm, she left the top buttons of her blouse undone, unaware that it hinted provocatively at her pretty shape.

On the stroke of six, Donna thumped the knocker on the sturdy wooden door of Jared's home. He opened the door looking every inch the cattle baron he was. His crisp black jeans and soft white chambray shirt sheathed the muscles of a body honed by hard physical labour.

In some relief Donna noted that he'd dispensed with those hideous shirts. Subtlety did everything for his image and she made so bold as to tell him so.

'Black and white,' she finished, 'is always a stunning combination, on a man as well as on a woman.'

Amusement glimmered in the grey eyes. He hadn't given his image a moment's thought, tearing into his clothes as soon as he'd come out of the shower.

'Why, thank you, Donna. It appears that I can be quite sensible when the mood takes me.'

Unsure whether he was laughing at her, Donna peeped up at him and agreed. 'I'm relieved to hear it.'

Jared's veiled glance took in every

detail of her appearance without seeming to notice her at all. It left him feeling breathless.

'You look . . . very nice, yourself.' He said it with the air of a man trying out words he'd not spoken in a long time, which was in fact the case.

When Donna looked up, it was to find him still staring at her, his eyes very bright. She cleared her throat. 'Yes. Well now that we have the courtesies out of the way, may I come in?'

Jared gave himself a mental shake and ushered her into the living-room where his small daughter immediately flung herself into Donna's arms.

'Hi, Miss McGuire,' Amy-Kate squeaked. 'Have you come for dinner?'

'Yes, Amy-Kate. I've also come to speak to you about some clothing for your Barbie dolls, remember?'

Amy-Kate looked blank. 'My Barbies?'

'Yes. Your father said . . . ' Donna turned accusing blue eyes on her host. 'Didn't you say something about clothing?'

Jared's gaze was rock-steady. 'Oh, that.'

He cleared his throat. 'I admit freely that it was a ruse to get you here for dinner. But now you're here, I am certain your advice would be most welcome. How 'bout fetching those dolls, Amy-Kate?'

Donna seated herself rather stiffly on the sofa, feeling both angry and confused. Angry because Jared was so arrogant as to think he could manipulate her, and confused because he so obviously desired her company.

'You're shameless, but now that I'm here,' she stated defiantly, 'I shall enjoy myself.'

At the table Amy-Kate was particularly careful to impress her new mamma with her good manners. For once she ate everything on her plate and politely requested to be excused when she'd finished.

Jared, undeceived by his daughter's sudden docility, gave an inward sigh. 'Yes, you may get down from the table, Amy-Kate.'

'Thank you, Daddy,' she told him

solemnly. She turned to Donna. 'When I've cleaned my teeth, Miss McGuire, will you tuck me up in bed?'

'I'd be delighted,' Donna agreed warmly.

True to her word, she went to the child's room after dinner and knelt beside the bed for prayers, pretending not to notice Amy-Kate's confidence that her entreaties to God for a new mamma would be answered soon and without fail.

Donna tucked her into bed and dropped a kiss on her cheek. 'Goodnight, sweetheart.'

'Goodnight, Miss McGuire. Would you like to be my new mamma? I'll be real good.' Her piping voice held a slight quaver.

Donna swallowed. 'You're a wonderful little girl and anyone would be honoured to be your mamma, Amy-Kate.'

'My new mamma would have to love my daddy, too.'

'Yes, she would.'

'Do you love my daddy, Miss McGuire?'

Donna was an honest girl. 'Well, no, not at the moment, Amy-Kate.'

'Could you start to love him soon? Just a little?'

Donna wondered how to let the child down gently. 'It's possible,' she said cautiously. 'Your father is a very attractive man and he has the most gorgeous eyes, hasn't he? And . . . and hair. It's dark and thick and it curls very nicely on his neck.'

'My daddy would take good care of you, Miss McGuire.'

'Yes,' Donna agreed slowly. She added in a rather surprised voice, 'I rather think he would. However, it's not going to happen. I am sure that there are many other ladies in Uvalde who would wish to marry him.'

'Like Bonny-Sue?'

'Er . . . yes. Like Miss Simpson.'

'I don't like Bonny-Sue, she's always phoning my daddy and buying him awful shirts, and she giggles!'

Donna hid a smile. With women like Bonny-Sue around, she couldn't help feeling a sneaking sympathy for Amy-Kate's father.

'Goodnight, honey.' She rose to put out the light, gathered up her shoes and made for the passage.

At the door she gave a small gasp as she collided with Jared's hard body which was propping up the doorpost.

Donna went hot with embarrassment. The wretch must surely have heard their every word.

'I'd like to go home now,' she told him quickly, 'I won't stay for coffee because I have to be up early . . .

'Ah, yes, so you do,' Jared agreed politely. He ushered her with almost unflattering haste to the front door and out to her car.

'Please thank Mrs Gonzales for her lovely meal,' Donna mumbled from the driver's seat.

He nodded. 'Will do.'

5

For the next few weeks Donna threw herself into her ranching with a sort of frenzied zeal, remembering her grandfather's adage, 'Hard work keeps the fences up.' Yes, hard work was the only way to make a success of her operation and she certainly wasn't afraid of hard work.

She saw nothing of Jared Jackson and his daughter, and whenever she thought of the night she'd dined with them and that bedtime conversation with Amy-Kate, her cheeks grew hot with embarrassment.

Jared had long since come to the conclusion that he didn't want to lose Donna, but the decision had been made against his better judgment. He needed more time. She was the sort of woman who would require a complete, no-holds-barred commitment.

'Hank, may I have a word with you?' Donna called as Hank emerged from the barn one morning. 'Come inside for a cup of coffee, it's almost time for a break.'

What she had to say would not be pleasant. They would both need that coffee by the time she'd finished.

The truth was, she'd been shocked and dismayed to find on her last visit to town that the tack and feed man, despite his saying he would consider it, had decided not to allow her any credit after all. Old Silas Wilson had been perfectly open about his prejudices.

'Ain't no job for a woman,' he growled cynically. 'Can't take the chance on you paying up, girl.' Besides, he'd had two warnings about her from that nice young man. Seems it was all about town what a bad payer she was.

So Donna had been forced to pay upfront for the next lot of supplies out of her savings, which had now dwindled alarmingly. Neither had she been able to get credit at the supermarket, and the freezer was almost empty. In fact, the manager had been downright unfriendly.

Donna sighed. She had exactly two hundred dollars to her name and Hank still had to be paid. 'Hank, we have a little difficulty.'

Hastily she explained the situation. 'I'll be able to pay you this week,' she told him as she handed over his pay packet, 'and then we must make some urgent decisions.' Her sapphire eyes dimmed with unhappiness. 'You may want to look for another job.'

Hank shook his head. 'This is my home, Missy. I'll work for nothing if need be, just to keep things going. It'll be all right, you'll see. You'll think of something.'

His confidence was gratifying, but try as she would no bright ideas emerged.

She drove into town the following day in order to collect some more veterinary supplies; a jar of liniment and rolls of thick white gauze for Beauty's leg, and a tube of equine shampoo for both horses who were looking considerably dusty despite constant grooming with a curry comb.

* * *

There was one parking space between the diner and the post office and Donna eased the car into it. Not for anything would she try to find parking behind the diner again. She needed to be able to keep a firm eye on the Dodge and anyone who came near it.

When her chores were completed she went into the diner for a cup of coffee so that she could ponder her problems in relative peace.

She could always take a job in town providing she could get one, but it would not be fair on Hank who would then have to shoulder all the ranching chores. It was hard enough as it was with just the two of them; they were doing the job of four men, at least.

Donna frowned as she flopped down on to the red banquette. If she was bone tired, how must Hank feel? He was becoming slower and slower. Wrestling a balking steer at the dipping chute was a hard job for an old man, and an even harder one for a woman who was unused to such exertions.

Cleaning the corral left her feeling exhausted, and as for pitching hay into the feeders, mired to the ankles in cattle dirt and with the flies buzzing around her head, life wasn't exactly a teaspoon of honey. She'd had no idea that ranching was such hard, dirty work!

For the first time since arriving in Texas Donna had to admit to a feeling of defeat, but being a plucky girl, she told herself briskly that it was still early days yet. Given time she could still make something of the McGuire Ranch, but it was a frustrating fact of life that without money there was little she could do to take the operation forward.

'Hi, honey,' Lacey greeted her with a smile. 'You're looking a little tired. Been working hard, I daresay. A nice cup of coffee . . . ?'

‘Please,’ Donna said gratefully. ‘And some of that apple pie, Lacey.’ Might as well be hanged for a sheep as for a lamb, she decided. That would leave her with exactly nineteen dollars.

Tyler Grey entered the diner and spotted Donna in the corner. With a wolfish grin he threaded his way between the tables to join her. ‘Afternoon, Donna. What brings you to town?’

Donna looked up from spooning sugar into her mug. ‘Oh, hello, Tyler. I came to get some more supplies.’

Without waiting to be invited he sat down opposite her and laid his sweat-stained cowboy hat on the seat beside him.

‘You’re one stubborn girl, aren’t you, Donna McGuire? Still keen on this ranching business, I see. Man, you should marry a rich man and live a life of leisure. Give up before you’re in over your head. You really mean to carry on?’

‘Yes.’

‘Why not reconsider? I could get you a good price, like I said,’ he coaxed.

'Two hundred thousand at least for the land, and then the buildings. They'd fetch —'

'No way,' Donna interrupted him shortly. 'I'd die before I gave up. I'd even consider taking a bank loan . . . '

She was annoyed with herself as soon as the words were out. It was none of Tyler's business how she financed her operation.

His gaze sharpened. 'That sounds like you're in financial difficulties. All the more reason to sell your land, honey. My good friend, Brock Haslam, he'll write you a cheque tomorrow.'

No need for the lady to know that it would be Tyler Grey who would write the cheque and purchase the land, he thought cunningly. He'd then sell it on to his friend, Brock, for four times as much — it's real worth, if the truth be told. Not that the truth would be told, because witless dames like Ms McGuire were there to be picked off, no kidding . . .

Donna finished the last of her pie

and put down her fork. 'No, thank you.' She reached for her sling bag and rose. Tyler rose, too. He did not care to be towered over by tall females.

'My advice to you, Donna, is to pack it in. But if you really are determined to remain in Uvalde I have a friend who could help you. Name of Bobby Rae Jones. He's the lending officer at the bank.'

Let the stupid girl think that he was on her side! He added encouragingly, 'If the bank won't oblige, come back to me, honey. That cheque'll be waiting . . . '

'When pigs fly,' Donna said forcefully. 'Goodbye, Tyler.'

'Who's taking my man's name in vain?' grinned Lacey as she cleared up the crockery. 'I heard you speaking about Bobby Rae Jones.'

'Donna here wants to ask him for a loan,' Tyler informed her, ignoring Donna's outraged face.

'In that case I'll put in a good word for you, Donna,' Lacey offered, and bustled off.

'Now that's what I call real friendly,'

Tyler observed, hiding his devious thoughts beneath a charming smile. He turned away so that Donna would not notice his glee. Tyler Grey would be having a word with Bobby Rae at the earliest opportunity . . .

Donna returned thoughtfully to the car. Despite her dislike and mistrust of Tyler, he had a point. If the bank would grant her a loan, even a small one, she could carry on. It couldn't do any harm to at least enquire, could it? In fact, it might do a power of good.

Filled with renewed hope, she marched up the street to the bank. 'Mr Jones will be able to see you on Friday at three o'clock,' his secretary informed her a few minutes later. 'Your name is . . . ?'

'Donna McGuire. It's in connection with a loan.'

'That's what they all say, honey. Y'all have a nice day, now.'

Donna rode home feeling much happier. There was still hope, after all.

* * *

For the rest of the week she threw herself confidently into her work. She and Hank dipped the steers, sterilised the birthing stalls, doctored Beauty's leg and made sure that Norman had his regular feeds.

The calf was improving daily and would soon have to be weaned on to hay before being returned to the north pasture. Friday came round before she knew it.

'I'll put on my best finery,' she informed a disinterested Codger as she climbed out of her working gear and went to take a shower. 'It's always a good idea to look prosperous when you speak to your bank manager!'

Half-an-hour later, in her new blue skirt and a crisp white Western-style shirt with its impressive fringe, she left the ranch. She'd taken particular pains with her hair and make-up, and the sparkle of anticipation in her eyes was still there when she parked her car in the main street and walked confidently into the bank.

'Mr Jones will be with you in a moment,' his secretary cooed, her plastic smile revealing her pristine dental work. 'Y'all just sit right down, now . . . '

Donna did as she was told and waited half-an-hour.

'Mr Jones will see you now, Miss McGuire.'

Annoyed at being kept waiting, but quelling her nervousness, Donna entered the room the secretary had indicated. She smiled confidently and held out her hand.

'Mr Jones? I'm Donna McGuire and I own the McGuire Ranch north of Uvalde. I'm very pleased to meet you.'

To her consternation Bobby Rae Jones was sitting with his snakeskin boots propped up on one corner of his desk, paging idly through an auto magazine. He appeared to be in no hurry.

'Sure you are, honey,' he smirked.

He slapped his feet on to the floor and uttered in a bored voice, 'Howdy, lady. What can I do for you? You'd better sit down.'

Donna hid her instant dislike of the man. As bank officer he was hardly presenting a good image for his company, behaving in this sloppy fashion and then gazing at her in the same way a hawk would view a small rodent in the grass.

Undeterred, Donna gazed back. Bobby Rae, she thought, looked like an ego-ridden, gone-to-seed wrestler; all self-importance and muscle-bound flab. What on earth did Lacey McCoy see in him?

'I am here to ask for a loan,' she began. 'I have with me a business plan for the McGuire Ranch.'

She reached into her sling bag and withdrew the document she'd spent all the previous evening putting together.

Bobby Rae stood up slowly and reached for it. He returned to his seat and gave it a cursory glance before tossing it on to his cluttered desk.

'I'll take a look at your proposals and then advise you on my decision,' he informed her importantly. 'How much would you be wantin' to borrow, Ma'am?'

Donna mentioned a sum. 'By this time next year the ranch should be showing a small profit and I shall be meticulous about repayments,' she assured him.

'Yes, well . . . ' he scratched the bridge of his nose. 'I'll be in touch, honey. My secretary will give you a call.' He looked her up and down in what she considered to be a rather insolent fashion before asking carelessly, 'You datin' anyone?'

Donna gave him an icy stare. 'That has nothing to do with the business in hand.'

He ushered her to the door. 'You'd be surprised, honey. You'd be surprised.'

Donna marched out, her cheeks pink with annoyance. Of all the loathsome males, and to think she'd been forced to beg him for money!

She cannoned straight into a solid

masculine chest and gasped as the breath left her lungs in a whoosh. 'Good afternoon, Donna,' Jared Jackson's deep voice sounded in her ear, 'it may be a good idea to look where you are going.'

Donna lifted her head quickly and her forehead met his chin with a crack, making his hat fly off backwards.

'Easy, honey . . . '

Embarrassed, she disentangled herself and looked up into his amused grey eyes. 'I'm really sorry. I . . . I just didn't see you.' She wished him a stiff good afternoon.

Jared retrieved his hat and shoved it back on to his dark hair. He stood aside to allow her to pass, scrutinising with interest her flushed, angry face. 'Don't let me keep you, Donna. You obviously aren't keen to spare the horses. You were coming at a double trot.'

Donna gave a prim nod and pushed past him, trying to steady her breathing. It wasn't the body blow as much as his proximity which was causing her some problems. Whenever she saw the man, he disturbed her immensely. He excited her, too.

Underneath that mocking exterior she suspected there was a very nice man. He'd been kind to her when her grandfather had died, and he was very sweet with his small daughter. If he wasn't quite so arrogant she'd even consider dating him.

As she left the banking hall she heard the secretary's nasal drawl telling Mr Jackson to take a seat because Mr Jones was tied up at present.

'Reading magazines,' Donna muttered in disgust.

She waited with a mixture of hope and dread for Bobby Rae Jones's telephone call. When it came, she found herself gripping the edge of the hall table in anticipation, but as she listened her face paled.

'Mr Jones regrets the bank is unable to offer you a loan,' his secretary announced in a disinterested voice. 'Y'all have a nice day, now . . . '

Donna thanked her as civilly as she could and slammed down the receiver. 'If I hear those words one more time, I shall scream,' she fumed, so that Codger, unused to such displays of temper, looked up in alarm.

It was time to begin making the evening meal, but Donna was past caring. She rushed out to the barn, quickly saddled Flint and galloped out of the yard. It took precisely twenty minutes to reach Jared Jackson's front door, by which time her anger was white hot.

Finding the nearest railing on which to tether the pony, she flung herself up the porch steps to the front door where she gave the knocker an almighty thump.

Mrs Gonzales, on her way to the kitchen to prepare the evening meal, paused with a startled face and went to see who it was. The boss had asked not to be disturbed, but this sounded urgent.

'Yes, Miss?'

'I wish to speak with Mr Jackson,' Donna told her in a voice which brooked no argument.

His housekeeper took one look at Donna's face and nodded. 'This way, Miss.'

She led Donna down the passage to the study door and knocked.

'Come in,' Jared invited tersely. He looked up impatiently from the computer monitor where he had been examining a spread sheet. 'What is it, Mrs Gonzales?'

'Miss McGuire wishes to see you, sir.'

Jared's gaze slid past his housekeeper to encounter Donna's furious face. He hid his surprise and rose slowly from his desk.

'Won't you come in, Donna McGuire? By the look on your face, honey, the roof's caved in on the henhouse.'

As soon as the door was closed, Donna rounded on him wrathfully. 'You know very well I do not keep hens. And I am not your honey! I will never be your honey. Jared Jackson; you are the most despicable man I have ever encountered.'

She snatched breath and plunged on furiously. 'If I were a man I'd knock you cold! I'd pin your hide to the barn door and then burn it down — '

Angry tears came into her eyes and she blinked them away impatiently. Her throat squeezed shut and because she was unable to utter another word she continued to glare at him, her expression saying it all.

A bland mask descended over Jared's features. His grey eyes, warmly indulgent a moment before, had turned to volcanic rock.

'Sit down, Donna,' he invited coldly. 'If the roof's not caved in on the henhouse then the bottom must have fallen out of the milk bucket. I am all ears.'

Donna ignored his invitation. She stood staring up at him, her eyes flashing with temper.

'Will you stop saying things like that? I don't possess a milk bucket, and this is no joke; I shall be ruined, and it's all your fault! You have no decency whatever.'

Jared's gaze sharpened. 'Ruined?'

'Yes, ruined! As in bankrupt and out of business. You know very well what I mean, Jared Jackson.'

'I can't say that I do, Donna McGuire. You'd better lay it on the line.'

'All right, I will. It's about that loan.'

He appeared genuinely surprised. 'What loan?'

'The loan from Bobby Rae Jones,' she spat.

'Let me get this straight. You went to the bank to ask Bobby Rae for a loan?'

'You know perfectly well that I did! How can I possibly carry on without one? I can't get credit anywhere in this lousy town. You're all a bunch of impossible male chauvinists and I'm just a woman on her own, trying to make headway in a male-dominated job, for crying out loud!'

Jared stared at her, comprehension

dawning. 'I take it the loan was refused?'

Donna threw her hands into the air. 'Don't play dumb, you . . . you rattlesnake! You were in the bank, remember? I bumped into you. You went in to see Bobby Rae right after me, you needn't deny it. It was you who persuaded him not to lend me the money, wasn't it? Admit it. Just so you could force me to concede defeat.

'You knew I'd have to give up ranching, didn't you? Then you'd get exactly what you wanted; I'd have to sell you the McGuire Ranch . . . ' tears spilled unashamedly down Donna's cheeks. She rushed on, past caring. 'I hate you, Jared Jackson. I never wish to set eyes on you again.'

Jared's mouth had fallen open. 'You think I'd do a thing like that?' he asked quietly.

'Yes. You'd stop at nothing to get what you want! And don't you ever let the air out of my tyres again!'

He clamped his jaw over the many

things he would have liked to have said, and similarly controlled the impulse to take her in his arms and tell her what a fiddle-footed little fool she was, prattling about tyres and the like. Instead, he flung open the study door.

'In that case, there is nothing further to be said. You may leave my house, Donna McGuire. Should you wish to sell me your land you can get in touch with my solicitor, Joseph Ridley — whom you have already met.'

In stiff silence he ushered her to the front door. 'Goodbye, Ma'am. I can't say it's been a pleasure.'

No pleasure at all, he reflected once he'd shut the door on Donna's forlorn, angry figure.

Ever since she'd come into his life she'd boiled his blood, disturbed his ordered days and robbed him of a decent night's sleep. She'd won his daughter's heart, and now the child was convinced there was a new mamma in the offing.

She'd stolen his heart, too, it had to

be said. But the woman was acting like a loon, quite bent on destroying his reputation in this town as an honest, fair-minded individual.

Jared returned to his study, looked out through the window at the approaching dusk and heaved a great sigh. To think he'd even considered marrying her!

It had been a real nice dream while it had lasted.

6

Her anger spent, Donna rode home in a sad frame of mind. Her eyes were so full of tears she hardly noticed the dust catching at the back of her throat or the way Flint stumbled over the boulders in the dusk.

'Cowgirls,' she admonished herself with a watery sniff, 'don't cry.'

Determined to hide her anguish from Hank, at least for another few days, she proceeded to get on with the evening chores just as usual.

While Hank dealt with Flint's needs, Donna hurried into the kitchen, opened a few cans and whipped up a passable stew, serving it with the preprepared mashed potato she'd found on the shelf. Canned peaches were hastily thrown into a dish, covered with a scone mixture, also from a box, and sprinkled with cinnamon. Shoving the dish into the oven to bake, she went to set the table.

'Beef stew and peach cobbler for afters, Hank,' she informed him brightly a few minutes later.

'That sounds mighty fine, Missy.' He nodded, noting the recent signs of tears on her face. He offered awkwardly, 'Old Hank'll wash the dishes afterwards.'

'Indeed you will not. You will sit in front of the television as usual until bedtime, and I'll bring you your coffee!'

Hank hid his relief and folded his tired old body on to a kitchen chair. He bent his head and said the blessing in a gruff voice, in no way deceived as to the cause of Donna's distress.

In the morning things would look brighter, Donna told herself as she climbed into her nightdress. She didn't expect to get much sleep that night, but as soon as her head touched the pillow she fell into an exhausted slumber, only to waken to the sound of the alarm at four o'clock the next morning.

It was time, she decided, to send

Norman back to the north pasture. He had grown into a strong little bull with a cheeky brown stare and a strong mind of his own. He'd be an asset to Jared's herd; a thought which gave her no pleasure at all.

After giving Norman his morning feed, she tossed him a bunch of hay and went inside to make the breakfast before Hank arrived.

He gave her a rather anxious look which caused her to say brightly, 'It's about time I took a dip in that water tank, Hank.

At mid-morning when it's really hot, I'll ride up to the pasture, if you could just help me with getting Norman into the pickup? I'd like to return him to the herd up there.'

'Sure thing, Missy. He's turned out a fine calf; you raised him well.'

After morning coffee, Hank roped Norman, loaded him into the Dodge pickup and drove him up the hill while Donna followed on Flint at a more leisurely pace. Once released, Norman, delighted to be amongst his own kind, scampered away into the distance.

Hank reversed the pickup through the metal gate and returned to the barn to clean the stable, leaving Donna to close the gate behind him. As she approached the water tank she was relieved to see that the herd was grazing some way off.

The tank was situated near the boundary with Jared's land, but thankfully none of his men were about. Donna tore off her clothing and hung it neatly on the fence.

She climbed up the ladder in her new, bright yellow bikini and hurled her overheated body into the water. It was deliciously cool. She turned on her back, closed her eyes and floated, enjoying the first bit of relaxation she'd had in weeks.

It gave her the opportunity to reflect on her situation and restore some measure of peace to her troubled emotions.

'Face facts, Donna McGuire,' she

muttered, 'it is simply not possible to carry on. You've done your best, but circumstances have been against you . . . and some people!'

It was better to be pragmatic than to hide her head in the sand. No matter how painful it was for her, she would sell the land to Jared, leaving Uvalde to make a new start, probably in one of the smaller towns like Fredericksburg or Kerrville.

No. That would be too close. She would have to go as far away as she could from Jared Jackson and sweet little Amy-Kate as she could.

There was still time, according to the stipulation in her grandfather's will, to collect that extra twenty thousand dollars each which she and Seonaid would inherit if she sold the ranch. She would not be left penniless, and for that she was extremely grateful.

Donna stood upright in the chest-high water and reluctantly decided that it was time to go back to the cabin to fix lunch. She peeped over the edge of the tank and uttered a small scream. Fifty or so steers were bunched around the water, watching curiously to see if the human invading their watering hole was any cause for concern.

Donna gazed back in horror. There was no way she was prepared to get out of the water with such an audience. Those horns not only looked vicious; when used they could be quite deadly.

'Shoo,' she ordered nervously.

The animals took not the slightest notice but continued to stare. One steer even ventured nearer to drink.

'Go away, do,' Donna begged in a frightened voice.

'Trouble, Ma'am?' Jared asked blandly from the other side of the fence.

Donna spun around. 'How long have you been watching me?'

He shrugged. 'Does it matter? I rode over to see what your animals were staring at.'

He urged his enormous black stallion closer to the fence removed his hat and waved it in the air.

'Skat!' he bellowed.

In five seconds flat, the steers had disappeared, falling over themselves to reach the far corner of the pasture.

'Thank you,' Donna said stiffly, climbing out of the water with as much dignity as she could muster.

Jared enjoyed her progress in unhurried silence before spurring his horse in the opposite direction. As he galloped away he lifted his hat.

'A real pleasure, Ma'am,' he muttered bitterly.

* * *

Donna drove into Fredericksburg the next day for an interview with Jasper Ridley, her grandfather's solicitor. He seemed pleased with her decision to sell the McGuire Ranch and promised to contact Jared Jackson with the news as soon as possible.

'I shall see to it that you receive a fair price for your land,' he assured her.

Donna nodded. 'There is one condition to the sale. I want my ranch hand, Hank Henderson, to be employed by Mr Jackson for as long as he desires to remain on the McGuire Ranch. He is to have light duties . . . '

If Mr Ridley was surprised at this he gave no sign. 'As you wish. Should Mr Jackson still wish to purchase your land, I shall have the documents ready for you to sign by next week.'

'Oh, he'll want to purchase, all right,' she told the lawyer bitterly.

She drove home to tell Hank of her decision, hoping that he wouldn't be too disappointed.

The old man took her hand and wrung it. 'Reckon you had no option, Missy. I thank you for thinking of me.'

'It's what my grandfather would have wanted,' she assured him, hiding her heartache beneath a reassuring smile. 'Would you look after Codger and Beauty and Flint? It would be unkind to take them away from the ranch.'

Hank seemed pleased. 'A real pleasure, Missy.'

All that remained, thought Donna as she climbed into bed that night, was to await the signing of the deed of sale and the transfer to the funds into her bank account.

In addition to the extra twenty thousand dollars she would receive, there would be quite a little nest egg, the thought of which made her feel quite dizzy. But until then it would be business as usual, with Hank's help.

Soon Jared's ranch hands would take over the work, but until that happened she would not neglect her duties. Never let it be said by Jared Jackson that she had been lazy or incompetent, which as no doubt just the sort of hateful, mocking thing he would say!

* * *

The transaction took place sooner than expected. Within three days, Joseph Ridley had telephoned to say he would visit her after calling in at the Double Circle for Mr Jackson's signature.

He arrived in his large black saloon, explained that Mr Jackson was offering her eighty thousand dollars for the land and a further two hundred for the buildings.

'Does that meet you're your approval, Ma'am?'

Donna gazed at him, speechless. 'But . . . that's too much!' According to Tyler Grey, she should be getting a lot less.

'Indeed, it is not, Ma'am. It's a fair offer and I advise you to take it.' He coughed. 'Mr Jackson has expressed the desire to take transfer of the property by the end of next week. He would like you to vacate the ranch by Wednesday.'

'Certainly,' she replied coldly.

She put her signature to the documents in a rather shaky hand, after which she offered the lawyer a cup of coffee. He refused politely, citing urgent matters requiring his attention at the office, and took his dignified leave.

Watching his saloon disappear down

the drive, Donna breathed a prayer of thanks that she had been spared Tyler Grey's unscrupulous dealings. To think he'd been prepared to defraud her by offering her that paltry sum!

Thankfully she now had enough money in her account to make her financially independent. She would be able to buy a little business somewhere and make a new start. But first she would telephone Seonaid and tell her what had happened . . .

Her sister expressed herself delighted that Donna had changed her mind. 'Nasty, dirty work, ranching.' She failed to keep the triumph from her voice. 'Can't understand why you even considered it. You can keep the money, love. I have plenty of my own.'

Donna went to bed that night with her head in the clouds. If a small and unexpected sadness arose at the thought that she would never see Jared or his daughter again, she quelled it ruthlessly. He was a hard-nosed, unfeeling, hateful man who had robbed her of her family home, and for that she would never forgive him!

On Wednesday morning Donna made sure that the cabin was as tidy as she'd found it, went to say goodbye to Hank and the animals, and loaded up her few possessions in the black Dodge. She intended to drive to San Antonio before nightfall and spend a few days in a hotel.

After all the hard work of the last few weeks, she reckoned she deserved a little pleasure, and it would be fun to visit the Alamo and other exciting places like the famed River Walk.

Tonight she intended to enjoy an unhurried meal in one of the riverside restaurants while she listened to a jazz band and watched the barges sail by.

She turned her mind to such pleasures as she drove away from the ranch, determined to shake off her feelings of depression. If it was indeed true that cowgirls didn't cry, she would not shed another tear.

Instead of turning east on Highway

90 towards San Antonio, Donna decided to drive to Matt's diner to say goodbye to her only friend, Lacey McCoy, first. She parked outside the diner and hurried inside, intending to drink a quick cup of coffee and be on her way.

Lacey spotted her and approached the table. 'Hi, Donna. I heard you've had to sell your ranch. I'm awful sorry about that loan not coming through.'

'It's not your fault that Bobby Rae refused me,' Donna assured her.

'Bobby Rae!' Lacey spat. 'Don't ever mention his name to me again. The man's a total creep, Donna. We're through.'

'Oh?'

'Man's a viper and that's a fact. I found out he was seeing both Bodie Roper and Bonny-Sue Simpson the same time he was seein' me. How's that for a two-timing rattlesnake?'

'Three-timing.' Donna nodded sympathetically. 'I can't bear deceitful men, either. It's a complete waste of time.'

'Talk about deceit — I did speak to

him about that loan of yours, but Tyler Grey had promised him a little kickback if he refused you. Tyler told Bobby Rae that if you couldn't get a loan you'd be forced to sell your land to him on the cheap, and then he'd sell it on to his friend, Brock, for four times as much. He promised Bobby Rae a nice little sum, I can tell you.'

Donna paled. 'Would . . . would you say that again?'

'Sure. Tyler was responsible for you not getting that loan and he bribed Bobby Rae to refuse you. He told Bobby Rae he'd been using a few dirty tricks to frighten you into selling . . . like blackening your name around town so you'd get no credit, and letting the air out of your tyres.

'All I can say is that both of them are complete losers. I must have been mad to date Bobby Rae in the first place. I've been telling my friends about it . . . it'll soon get around how despicable they are. Coffee, you said . . . ?'

Donna jumped up. 'I won't have that

coffee after all, Lacey. I came to say goodbye, but I'll keep in touch.'

'Sure thing. Best of luck, Donna.' She bustled away.

Donna's hand shook badly as she inserted the key into the ignition. Her leg fared no better as she stomped on the accelerator. She felt like being sick!

Never in her life had she misjudged someone as badly as she'd misjudged Jared Jackson. He was a decent, caring, hard-working man, and to think she'd accused him like a fishwife, when all along it had been Tyler Grey's doing!

Decisively she swung the Dodge around and headed out of town, straight back in the direction she'd come from. Being a girl of integrity she refused to leave without apologising to Jared, no matter how difficult it would be. Donna McGuire had always been True Blue, and she wasn't changing now.

* * *

It was almost lunchtime when she turned into the dusty road leading to the Double Circle. Amy-Kate would be at school and Mrs Gonzales would be about to serve the lunch.

It was embarrassing to arrive just as Jared would be sitting down to his midday meal, but what she had to say would not take long.

Donna cut the engine and sat for a moment in order to gather her courage. Then taking a deep breath, she slammed the car door and marched up to the house.

Jared was not sitting down to a substantial midday meal. He was in the kitchen cutting himself a large hunk of bread and cheese. With a sound of impatience he flung down the knife, wiped his hands on a tea towel and went to answer the door.

'Donna McGuire,' he acknowledged coldly. His unenthusiastic glance flicked her up and down. 'What can I do for you this time?'

Donna swallowed. 'May I come in?'

Reluctantly he stood aside. 'I'm about to eat my lunch. Kindly say what you have to say.'

Donna stepped into the hall. It didn't look quite as pristine as usual. There was dust on the carved table and the rug was crooked. One of Amy-Kate's books and two Barbie dolls were lying on the floor together with a pair of Jared's socks.

Donna cleared her throat, not quite knowing where to begin.

'Well?' he demanded.

She lifted her chin. 'I was mistaken in believing you to be the unscrupulous man I accused you of being. I have just discovered it was not you who influenced the outcome of that loan. I have come to apologise before I go.'

Jared's face was inscrutable. 'Well, well, well . . . ' he said softly.

'I . . . I heard from Lacey McCoy in Uvalde this morning that it was really Tyler Grey who bribed Bobby Rae to refuse my loan and let down my tyres. I'm sorry I misjudged you.'

She added nervously, 'I couldn't go without saying how sorry I am. I'll go now. Goodbye.' She turned and headed for the door.

Jared was there before her, standing with his back against the sturdy, dark wood. 'Apology accepted, Donna.'

'Thank you. If you'll excuse me . . . ?'

He cleared his throat. 'There is no need to rush off.'

'There's every need. It's lunchtime.'

'Sure, and I was just makin' myself a sandwich and a cup of coffee. Will you join me?'

Hunger had been gnawing in the pit of her stomach. It overcame her better judgement. 'Would Mrs Gonzales mind?'

'Mrs Gonzales has resigned. She left on Monday. Went to look after her two grandchildren since her daughter's fallen ill.'

He took her arm and jerked his head towards the kitchen. 'Will cheese do?'

'Cheese would be great.'

* * *

Jared made short work of preparing the sandwiches while Donna watched him, feeling a little awkward at accepting his hospitality, but it was too late now. She would leave as soon as she had eaten.

But Jared, it seemed, had other ideas. He rose from the table, ushered her into the living room and asked, 'What are your immediate plans?'

Donna told him.

He eyed her thoughtfully. 'Would you consider helping me out of my . . . er, present difficulty?'

'What difficulty?'

'I need a housekeeper.' He managed to sound quite plaintive. 'I'm not much of a cook.'

At her doubtful look, he added quickly, 'Amy-Kate is lonely, she needs supervision in the afternoons. I simply haven't the time.' He named a salary far beyond the going rate. 'Just for a few weeks until I can find someone else,' he coaxed.

Donna chewed her lip, unable to decide. It was very tempting. If she stayed, she would see him every day and perhaps he would fall a little in love with her.

'I couldn't possibly work for a man who wears deplorable shirts,' she told him at length.

Jared looked down at his offensive apparel. 'I could always ditch it.'

'You'll have to. It's quite the loudest monstrosity I've ever seen. Did Bonny-Sue give it to you?'

Quick as the snap of a bullwhip, Jared undid the buttons and whipped off his shirt.

'That better?' he enquired blandly.

Donna raised her eyes to heaven. 'Purple underwear!'

Jared glanced sheepishly at his T-shirt. 'It used to be white but it ran in the wash.'

'What you need,' Donna told him in exasperation, 'is a wife!'

Jared stroked his chin, pretending to consider. 'You have a valid point there. Will you marry me, Donna?'

She gaped. 'You . . . you can't be serious?'

'Yup. I'm serious.'

Donna peeped up into his face and what she saw there changed the situation entirely. 'You really are serious,' she marvelled.

'Sure I am, honey. As I see it, you've got two options — be my housekeeper, or be my wife. Work for me, or marry me.'

'They both amount to the same thing,' she pointed out with a grin.

His mouth twitched. 'One way or the other, I'm not letting you out of my life, Donna-Marie McGuire. Besides, I know you're a hard worker. You did pretty well these past few weeks.'

'Well, that's something, at least.'

'So what do you say?'

'I don't love you,' she told him, avoiding his eyes. She might be True Blue, but she was entitled to a little fib once in a while in the interests of deciding her future.

'Maybe not, but I love you.'

Her head snapped up. 'What did you say?'

'I love you, Donna McGuire. I've loved you for weeks. I just had to clear it with myself first, that's all.'

'Well . . . why didn't you say so?'

'Honey, I was working' up to it. Then you went and threw that hissy fit about your loan. I figured you thought I was lower'n in a snake's belly. Rattlesnake, to be exact.'

Donna blushed. Had she really said that?

'I was wrong,' she admitted humbly. 'Will you forgive me?'

Jared grinned. 'No sweat.'

His grey eyes grew serious. 'I'm a simple man, Donna. When I make a commitment, I stick to it. I want to make a commitment to you and stick to it for the rest of my life. Honey, I don't know how else to say it.'

He watched the amazement of her face and continued, 'But if you won't marry me or work for me, I might as well put this on again.'

He reached for the garish garment he'd thrown on the floor.

Donna watched in fascination as he shrugged it on, his strong, tanned fingers dealing nimbly with the buttons.

'Hold it, Buster,' she ordered.

He slanted an eyebrow at her. 'You have a problem?'

Donna pretended to think. 'Let's not rush into any hasty decisions, here.'

She paused. 'I'll work for you as your housekeeper for three months,' she told him cautiously, 'and we'll take it from there.'

Jared hid his jubilation. At least she wasn't turning him down flat. Half a loaf was better than none.

'Fine.' He nodded. 'May I kiss my housekeeper in order to seal the deal?'

'Surely that's a little unusual?'

'Not in my house.' Without waiting for her reply, he took her into his arms and kissed her thoroughly, taking his time about it.

'Perhaps,' Donna told him thoughtfully when she'd regained her breath, 'we'll make it one month instead of three.'

He kissed her again. 'One week.'

Donna choked. How like a man! 'A week doesn't give me long enough to choose a wedding gown. Besides, the colours have to be perfect for the whole party.'

Jared knew when to give in gracefully. 'Two weeks then,' he said firmly, 'no longer.'

Two weeks, he figured, would be just about right. It would give him ample time to see Joseph Ridley about the title deeds to the McGuire Ranch.

They would make a fitting wedding gift for his bride so that she need never again part with her inheritance.

'Two weeks it is,' Donna agreed, wondering if she were losing her mind but feeling deliciously happy about it.

'I'll have Lacey McCoy as my bridesmaid . . . in deep blue, of course, with pink rosebuds and creamy baby's breath. Amy-Kate will be the little flower girl . . . '

At the thought of Amy-Kate she gave a little gasp. 'It's time to fetch her from school, surely?'

Jared checked his watch and nodded. 'So it is.'

With a happy laugh, Donna grabbed him by the hand. 'Then let's go together and introduce her to her new mamma.'

* * *

Jared closed his eyes briefly as he breathed a silent prayer of thanks. His loneliness was at an end, and Amy-Kate at last had her heart's desire.

He determined to make Donna fall madly in love with him, although his intuition told him she was already halfway there.

'Anything you say, Ma'am,' he told her with a grin. 'But first I'd like to kiss my housekeeper one more time.'

Donna went into his arms knowing without a doubt that this was the cowboy she'd come all the way to Texas for.

We do hope that you have enjoyed reading this large print book.

Did you know that all of our titles are available for purchase?

We publish a wide range of high quality large print books including:
Romances, Mysteries, Classics
General Fiction
Non Fiction and Westerns

Special interest titles available in large print are:
The Little Oxford Dictionary
Music Book, Song Book
Hymn Book, Service Book

Also available from us courtesy of Oxford University Press:
Young Readers' Dictionary
(large print edition)
Young Readers' Thesaurus
(large print edition)

For further information or a free brochure, please contact us at:
Ulverscroft Large Print Books Ltd.,
The Green, Bradgate Road, Anstey,
Leicester, LE7 7FU, England.
Tel: (00 44) **0116 236 4325**
Fax: (00 44) **0116 234 0205**

Other titles in the
Linford Romance Library:

DARK MOON

Catriona McCuaig

When her aunt dies, Jemima is offered a home with her stern uncle, but vows to make her own way in the world by working at a coaching inn. She falls for the handsome and fascinating Giles Morton, but he has a menacing secret that could endanger them both. When Jemima is forced to choose between her own safety and saving the man she loves, she doesn't hesitate for a moment — but will they both come out of it alive?

HOME IS WHERE THE HEART IS

Chrissie Loveday

Jayne and Dan Pearson have moved to their dream house . . . a huge dilapidated heap on top of a Cornish cliff. The stresses of city life are behind them, their children consider their new home 'the coolest house ever', and the family's future looks rosy. But when a serious accident forces them to re-think their dream, they embark upon a completely different way of life — though its pleasures and disasters bring a whole new meaning to the word *stress* . . .